FUN學
美國各學科初級課本
新生入門英語閱讀 二版

4

AMERICAN
SCHOOL
TEXTBOOK

Reading Key BASIC

如何下載 MP3 音檔

❶ 寂天雲 APP 聆聽：掃描書上 QR Code 下載「寂天雲－英日語學習隨身聽」APP。加入會員後，用 APP 內建掃描器再次掃描書上 QR Code，即可使用 APP 聆聽音檔。

❷ 官網下載音檔：請上「寂天閱讀網」（www.icosmos.com.tw），註冊會員／登入後，搜尋本書，進入本書頁面，點選「MP3 下載」下載音檔，存於電腦等其他播放器聆聽使用。

MP3

寂天雲 APP

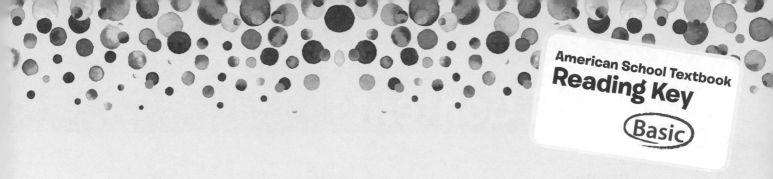

The Best Preparation for Building Academic Reading Skills and Vocabulary

The Reading Key series is designed to help students to understand American school textbooks and to develop background knowledge in a wide variety of academic topics. This series also provides learners with the opportunity to enhance their reading comprehension skills and vocabulary.

- **Reading Key <Basic 1–4>** is a four-book series designed for beginning learners.

- **Reading Key <Volume 1–3>** is a three-book series designed for beginner to intermediate learners.

- **Reading Key <Volume 4–6>** is a three-book series designed for intermediate to high-intermediate learners.

- **Reading Key <Volume 7–9>** is a three-book series designed for high-intermediate learners.

Features

- A wide variety of topics that cover American school subjects
- Intensive practice for reading skill development
- Building vocabulary through school subjects and themed texts
- Graphic organizers for each passage
- Captivating pictures and illustrations related to the topics

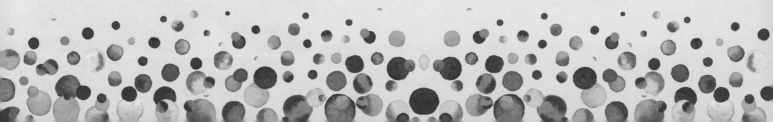

Table of Contents

Component

• Workbook

Syllabus Vol. 4

Subject	Topic & Area	Title
Social Studies ★ **History and Geography**	World Geography & Culture World Geography & Culture Our Earth and Resources Our Earth and Resources	Countries in the World The World's Best Earth Is Our Home Recycle, Reuse, and Reduce
Science	A World of Animals Our Earth Health Health	A World of Animals: Bears Earthquakes The Food Pyramid Staying Healthy
Language ★ **Mathematics** ★ **Visual Arts** ★ **Music**	Language Arts Computation Visual Arts A World of Music	Where Is It? Addition and Subtraction Sculptures A World of Instruments

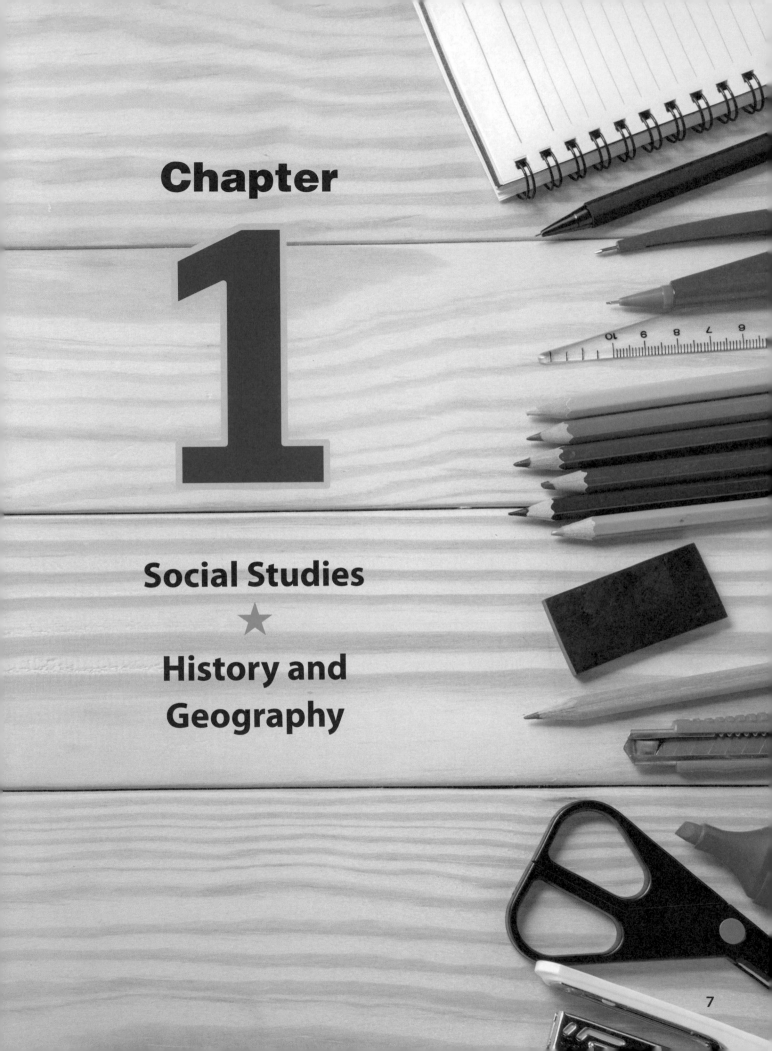

Chapter

1

Social Studies

★

History and Geography

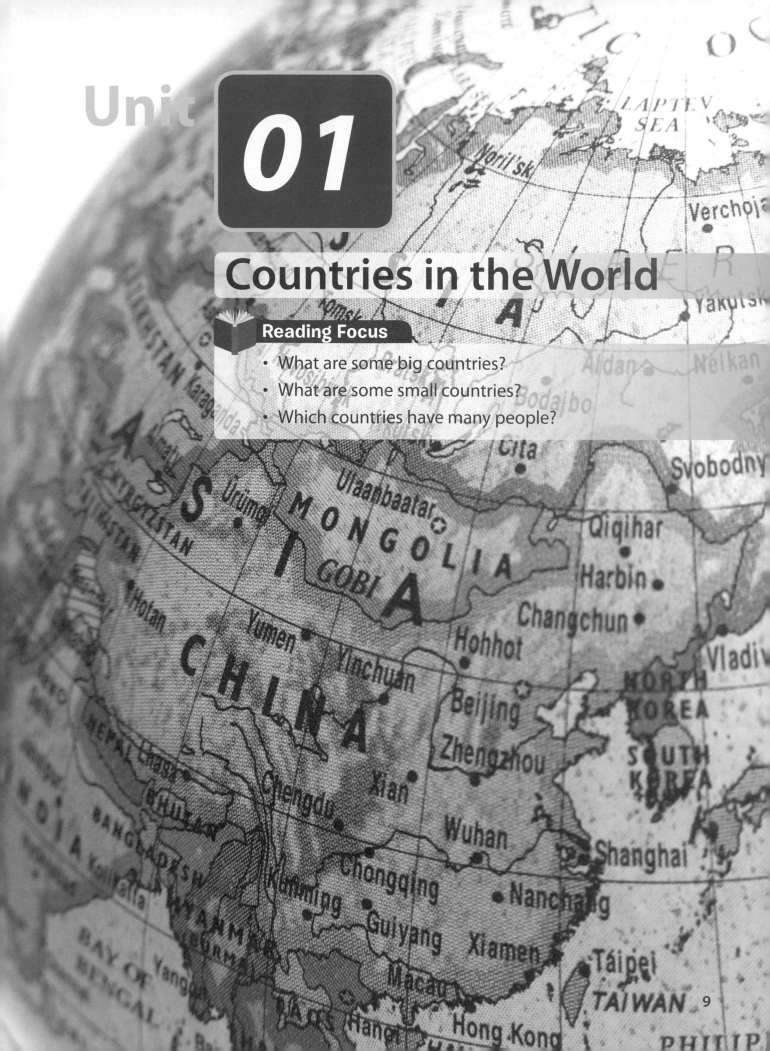

Unit

01

Countries in the World

📖 **Reading Focus**

- What are some big countries?
- What are some small countries?
- Which countries have many people?

9

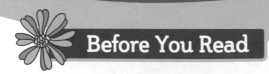

Before You Read

 01

Key Words

The World's Biggest Countries

the 1st — **Russia**

the 2nd — **Canada**

the 3rd — **the United States**

the 4th — **China**

the 5th — **Brazil**

The World's Smallest Countries

the 1st — **Vatican City**

FRANCE

ITALY

Rome

the 2nd — **Monaco**

Power Verbs

be located
Vatican City **is located** in Rome.

live in
1.39 billion people **live in** China.

follow
You should **follow** the law.

Word Families: Words for Countries

population

100	hundred
1,000	thousand
1,000,000	million
1,000,000,000	billion

(national) flag

national anthem

country

law

language

culture

Countries in the World

How many countries are there in the world?
There are 193 countries in the world.

Some are big. Some are small.
Russia is the biggest country in the world.
Canada is the second biggest country in the world.
The United States is the third biggest country in the world.
And China and Brazil are the fourth and fifth biggest countries.

What is the smallest country in the world?
It is Vatican City.
It is located inside the city of Rome, Italy.
It is no bigger than a city block.
It has a tiny population, too.
Only about 1,000 people live in Vatican City.

▲ Vatican City is no bigger than a city block.

Which country has the biggest population?
China has the biggest population in the world.
About 1.39 billion people live in China.
India has more than 1.3 billion people.
The United States has more than 300 million people.

▲ China has the biggest population in the world.

Every country has its own flag.
It has a national anthem, too.
People in a country follow the same laws.
They speak the same language.
And they have the same culture.

▲ Every country has its own culture.

Check Understanding

1 **Which country does each picture show?**

_____   _____

2 **What is the biggest country in the world?**
   a Canada   **b** China   **c** Russia

3 **What is the smallest country in the world?**
   a Rome   **b** Vatican City   **c** Brazil

4 **Which country has the biggest population in the world?**
   a the United States   **b** China   **c** India

• **Answer the questions below.**

1 What are the five biggest countries in the world?
   ⇨ They are _____, _____, the _____ _____, China, and _____.

2 What is the smallest country in the world?
   ⇨ _____ _____ is the _____ country in the world.

Vocabulary and Grammar Builder

A **Look, Read, and Write.**
Look at the pictures. Write the correct words.

| billion | countries | flag | located |

 1 ▶ There are 193 _____ in the world.

 2 ▶ Vatican City is _____ inside Rome.

 3 ▶ About 1.39 _____ people live in China.

 4 ▶ Every country has its own _____.

B **The First or Second?**
Draw a circle around the right words and then write the words.

1 Canada is the _____ biggest country in the world.
   first   second

2 The United States is the _____ biggest country in the world.
   second   third

3 China is the _____ biggest country in the world.
   fourth   fifth

4 Brazil is the _____ biggest country in the world.
   fourth   fifth

02

The World's Best

Reading Focus

- What is the world's tallest mountain?
- What is the world's longest river?
- What is the world's largest desert?

Key Words

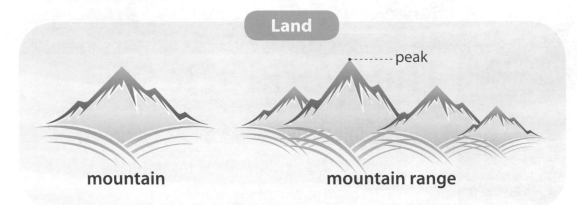

Land

mountain   peak   mountain range

Water

the Nile River

the Amazon River

the Mediterranean Sea

waterfall

Desert

the Sahara Desert

the Arabian Desert

the Gobi Desert

Power Verbs

rise
That mountain **rises** high.

stretch
The Andes **stretch** very long.

the Andes

flow
The river **flows** to the sea.

fall
The waterfall **falls** 807m.

Word Families

some

others

Some are low.
Others are high.

one

another

The Sahara is **one** huge desert.
The Gobi is **another** huge desert.

the Himalayas

Mountain
Ranges

the Andes

the Alps

the Rockies

The World's Best

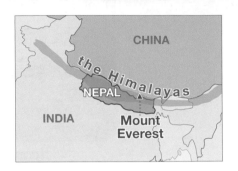

There are many mountains around the world.
Some are low. Others are high.

Mount Everest is the world's tallest mountain.
It rises 8,850 meters high.
It is located in the Himalayas on the
border of Nepal and China.
People call it "The Top of the World."

The Andes Mountains are the world's longest mountain range.
They stretch 7,000km long.
They are located in South America.

In Europe, there are the Alps.
Mont Blanc is the highest peak in the Alps.

The world's longest river is the Nile River.
It is in Africa.
It flows into the Mediterranean Sea.
The Amazon River is another huge river.
It is in South America.
It flows across Brazil to the Atlantic Ocean.

▲ the Amazon River

The world's largest desert is the Sahara in Africa.
Next is the Arabian Desert in the Middle East.
The Gobi Desert in Asia is another huge desert.

18

The world's highest waterfall is Angel Falls.
It falls 807m.
It is in Venezuela in South America.

▶ Angel Falls

Check Understanding

1 What does each picture show?

a

b

_____   _____

2 What is called "The Top of the World"?

a Mount Everest   b Mont Blanc   c the Andes

3 What is the highest peak in the Alps?

a Andes Mountains   b Mont Blanc   c Himalayas

4 The largest desert in the world is _____.

a the Gobi Desert   b the Sahara Desert   c the Arabian Desert

• **Answer the questions below.**

1 Where are the Andes Mountains?
  ⇨ They are in _____ _____.

2 What is the world's highest waterfall?
  ⇨ It is _____ _____ in _____, South America.

Vocabulary and Grammar Builder

A **Look, Read, and Write.**
Look at the pictures. Write the correct words.

peak　　　huge　　　Himalayas　　　border

1  ▶ Mount Everest is in the

_____.

2  ▶ The Himalayas are on the

_____ of Nepal and China.

3  ▶ Mont Blanc is the highest _____ in the Alps.

4 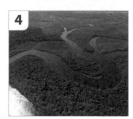 ▶ The Amazon River is another _____ river.

B **Rise or Stretch?**
Draw a circle around the right words and then write the words.

1　Mount Everest _____ high.
　　　　　　rises　　stretches

2　The Andes Mountains _____ very long.
　　　　　　　　rise　　stretch

3　The Nile River _____ into the Mediterranean Sea.
　　　　　　falls　　flows

4　Angel Falls _____ 807m.
　　　　　falls　　flows

Unit

03

Earth Is Our Home

Reading Focus

- What do we need to live?
- What are some natural resources?
- How do we use natural resources?

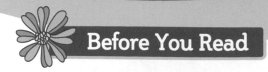

Key Words

Natural Resources

water

air

land

tree

oil

coal

fruits

paper

Things from Trees

furniture

house

Power Verbs

need
We **need** water to live.

use
We **use** water every day.

wash
We **wash** clothes.

cook
We **cook** food.

breathe
We **breathe** air.

disappear
The trees will **disappear**.

Word Families

living things

people

plants

animals

clean
The water is **clean**.

dirty
The water is **dirty**.

waste
Don't **waste** water.

save
Save water.

Earth Is Our Home 🎧 06

Look at the pictures.
How are they using water?

We need water to live.
We use water to drink.
We use water to grow food.
We use water to wash clothes and to cook food.

Plants also need water to grow.
And animals need water to live, too.
Without water, all living things cannot live.

We need air to breathe.
When the water and air are not clean, we cannot use them.
We need to keep the water and air clean.

Water and air are natural resources.
Natural resources come from nature.
Air, water, and land are important natural resources.

Trees are another natural resource.
We make many things from trees.
We also use the fruits from trees.

▲ Trees are important natural resources.

Earth is our home.
We use natural resources every day.
We should not waste our natural resources.
If we do not save our natural resources,
they will disappear.

Check Understanding

1 **Which natural resource does each picture show?**

_____   _____

2 **What do you need to wash clothes?**
   a land   **b** water   **c** air

3 **Where do natural resources come from?**
   a space   **b** sky   **c** nature

4 **We should not _____ our natural resources.**
   a use   **b** save   **c** waste

- **Answer the questions below.**

1 What natural resources should we keep clean?
   ⇨ We should keep the _____ and _____ clean.

2 What will happen if we do not save our natural resources?
   ⇨ They will _____.

Vocabulary and Grammar Builder

A **Look, Read, and Write.**
Look at the pictures. Write the correct words.

| need clean save natural resources |

1 ▸ Living things _____ water to live.

2 ▸ Water and land are _____ _____.

3 ▸ We need to keep the water _____.

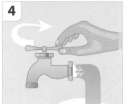
4 ▸ We should _____ our natural resources.

B **Drink or Wash?**
Draw a circle around the right words and then write the words.

1 We _____ water.
    drink   wash

2 People _____ air.
    drink   breathe

3 People _____ clothes with water.
    wash   make

4 People should not _____ resources.
    save   waste

Unit

04

Recycle, Reuse, and Reduce

Reading Focus

- What things can you recycle?
- What things can you use again?
- What things can you use less of?

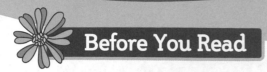

Key Words

paper

can

plastic

We Recycle!

glass

bottle

Paper

| newspaper | magazine | bag | box |

Power Verbs

recycle
Recycle cans.

reuse
Reuse boxes.

reduce
Reduce! Use less paper.

collect
We **collect** paper
every week.

put into
Put the glass **into**
the recycling bin.

turn off
Turn off the water.

Word Families

 trash ➡  trash can

 recycling things ➡ recycling bin

 less ⬌  more

29

Recycle, Reuse, and Reduce

My name is Susan.
Our class is learning how to save natural resources.
We can recycle, reuse, and reduce.
This makes less trash.
It also helps save natural resources.

First, we can recycle many things.
Our class collects things every Monday.
Here is what our class collects.
We collect paper.
We collect cans.
We collect plastic.
We collect glass.

Then, we put them into a recycling bin.
These things can be made into new things.
Then, we can use them again and again.

We can also reuse paper.
We write on both sides.
We save bags and boxes.
Then, we reuse them.

▼ We can recycle many things.

paper　　cans　　plastic　　glass

We can also reduce what we use.

When you brush your teeth, turn off the water.

When you leave a room, turn off the lights.

Check Understanding

1 **Which kind of recycling things does each picture show?**

a

b

_____ _____

2 **What does recycling do?**

a It makes less trash.　　b It makes more trash.　　c It makes fewer cans.

3 **How can we reuse paper?**

a write on one side　　　b write on both sides　　　c do not write on it

4 **When you brush your teeth, turn _____ the water.**

a off　　　　　　　　　b in　　　　　　　　　　　c on

- **Answer the questions below.**

1 What things can we collect?

⇨ We can collect _____, _____, _____, and _____.

2 What should we do when we leave a room?

⇨ We should _____ off the _____.

Vocabulary and Grammar Builder

A **Look, Read, and Write.**
Look at the pictures. Write the correct words.

> recycle   collect   turn off   put

1 ▸ We _____ paper every week.

2 ▸ We can _____ many things.

3 ▸ We _____ them into the recycling bin.

4 ▸ When you brush your teeth, _____ the water.

B **Less or More?**
Draw a circle around the right words and then write the words.

1 Recycling makes _____ trash.
less   more

2 We can save bags and boxes to _____ them.
reuse   reduce

3 We can also _____ what we use.
reduce   waste

4 When you leave a room, turn _____ the lights.
on   off

A Look at the pictures. Write the correct words.

billion   Himalayas   recycle   natural resources

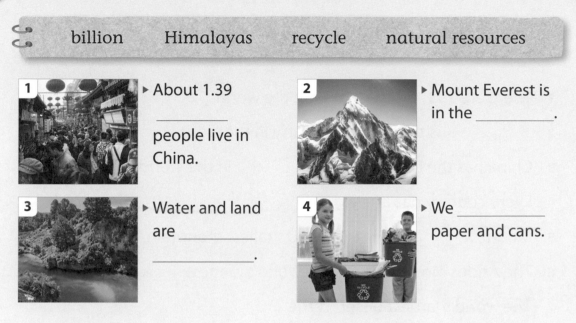

1 ▸ About 1.39 _____ people live in China.

2 ▸ Mount Everest is in the _____.

3 ▸ Water and land are _____ _____.

4 ▸ We _____ paper and cans.

B Draw a circle around the right words and then write the words.

 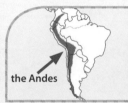

the Andes

1   The United States is the _____ biggest country in the world.
    second   third

2   The Andes _____ very long.
    rise   stretch

3   People _____ air.
    drink   breathe

4   Recycling can _____ natural resources.
    save   waste

C Complete the sentences with the words below.

| countries | population | Russia | national anthem |
| Everest | waterfall | Sahara | mountain range |

1 There are 193 _____ in the world.

2 _____ is the biggest country in the world.

3 China has the biggest _____ in the world.

4 Every country has a _____.

5 Mount _____ is the world's tallest mountain.

6 The Andes Mountains are the world's longest _____.

7 The world's largest desert is the _____.

8 The world's highest _____ is Angel Falls.

D Complete the sentences with the words below.

| need | clean | turn off | reuse |
| disappear | collects | save | living things |

1 We _____ water to live.

2 Without water, all _____ cannot live.

3 We need to keep the water and air _____.

4 If we do not save our natural resources, they will _____.

5 We can recycle, _____, and reduce.

6 Our class _____ paper and cans.

7 Recycling helps _____ natural resources.

8 When you leave a room, _____ the lights.

Chapter

2

Science

Unit

05

A World of Animals: Bears

Reading Focus

- What does a bear look like?
- What are some kinds of bears?
- Where do bears live?

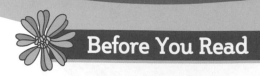

Key Words

Bears

polar bear

giant panda

brown bear

black bear

grizzly bear

sun bear

A Bear's Body Parts

ears

eyes

snout

fur

paw

claw

Power Verbs

be called
A baby bear **is called** a cub.

drink milk
Cubs **drink milk** from their mothers.

grow up
Bears leave home when they **grow up**.

find
Bears **find** winter homes.

sleep
Bears **sleep** in the winter.

move
Bears do not **move** during the winter.

Word Families: The Places Bears Live

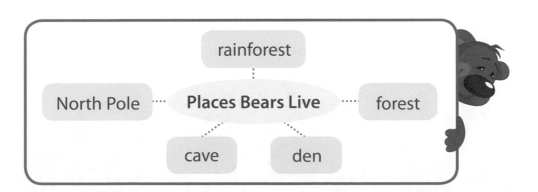

rainforest

North Pole ···· **Places Bears Live** ···· forest

cave   den

Bears 🎧 10

Look at the bears.
Bears have fur on their bodies.
It can be black, brown, or white.
Bears have paws and sharp claws.

A baby bear is called a cub.
Bear cubs are tiny when they are born.
They drink milk from their mothers.
When cubs grow up, they leave their mothers.

▲ Bears have fur on their bodies.

Bears live in dens.
Bears eat all kinds of food.
Some bears even hunt fish.

◄ hunting fish

The polar bear is the biggest bear in the world.
It lives near the North Pole.

The sun bear is the smallest bear in the world.
It lives in rainforests.

The giant panda lives in China.
It has black and white fur.

▲ The giant panda has black
and white fur.

The brown bear lives in many parts of the world.
The grizzly bear lives in North America.

In the late fall, many bears find winter homes.

They sleep during the winter.

They do not eat, drink, or move during the winter.

▲ Bears sleep during the winter.

Check Understanding

1 **Which type of bear does each picture show?**

a

b

_____   _____

2 **What do bears have on their bodies?**
   a feathers   b scales   c fur

3 **What is the biggest bear in the world?**
   a the polar bear   b the sun bear   c the brown bear

4 **A _____ is a bear's home.**
   a cub   b den   c paw

- **Answer the questions below.**

1 Where does the giant panda live?
   ⇨ The giant panda _____ in _____.

2 What do bears do in the winter?
   ⇨ They _____ during the winter.

Vocabulary and Grammar Builder

A **Look, Read, and Write.**
Look at the pictures. Write the correct words.

cub   panda   dens   claws

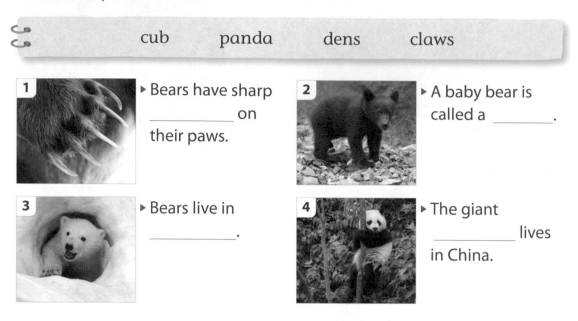

1 ▸ Bears have sharp _____ on their paws.

2 ▸ A baby bear is called a _____.

3 ▸ Bears live in _____.

4 ▸ The giant _____ lives in China.

B **Where Do They Live?**
Draw a circle around the right words and then write the words.

1 The polar bear lives near the _____.
North Pole   South Pole

2 The sun bear lives in _____.
deserts   rainforests

3 The giant panda lives in _____.
China   Chile

4 The grizzly bear lives in _____.
North America   South America

42

Unit

06

Earthquakes

Reading Focus

- What is an earthquake?
- What is a tsunami?
- How are earthquakes dangerous?

43

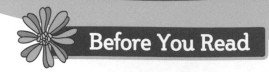

 11

Key Words

Earthquake

ground

ocean floor

shaking

large sea wave

cracks

tsunami

huge damage

Richter scale

Power Verbs

shake
The ground **shakes**.

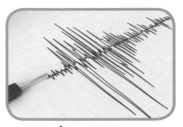

happen
Earthquakes often **happen**.

make cracks
Earthquakes **make cracks** in the ground.

destroy
Earthquakes can **destroy** buildings.

kill
Earthquakes can **kill** people.

cause
An earthquake can **cause** a tsunami.

hit
A huge tsunami **hit** Japan.

measure
The earthquake **measured** 9.5.

45

Earthquakes

Rumble! The ground starts to shake.
Everything on the ground shakes.
This is an earthquake.

Earthquakes happen every day.
But most earthquakes are very small.
So people do not feel these earthquakes.

Some earthquakes can be very big.
Big earthquakes can make cracks in the ground.
They can destroy buildings.
And they can kill many people, too.

▲ Some earthquakes can make cracks in the ground and destroy buildings.

Some earthquakes happen under the ocean floor.
Many of them cause a large sea wave.
This is called a tsunami.
A tsunami can cause huge damage.

In 2011, there was a big earthquake in Japan.
A huge tsunami hit northeastern Japan.
It killed thousands of people.

In 2004, a large tsunami hit Indonesia, too.
It killed more than 200,000 people.

The biggest earthquake was in 1960.
It happened in Chile.
It measured 9.5 on the Richter scale.

▲ Earthquakes are measured on the Richter scale.

Check Understanding

1   Which type of event does each picture show?

a

b

_____   _____

2   How often do earthquakes happen?

a every day   b once a week   c once a month

3   What is a tsunami?

a a large earthquake   b a large sea wave   c a large rainstorm

4   The biggest earthquake happened in _____.

a Indonesia   b Japan   c Chile

- **Answer the questions below.**

1   What can earthquakes do?
   ⇨ They can make _____ in the ground and _____ buildings.

2   What happened in 2011?
   ⇨ A _____ _____ hit northeastern Japan.

A **Look, Read, and Write.**
Look at the pictures. Write the correct words.

> shakes   Indonesia   cause   tsunami

1 ▸ An earthquake _____ the ground.

2 ▸ An underwater earthquake can cause a _____.

3 ▸ A tsunami can _____ huge damage.

4 ▸ A large tsunami hit _____ in 2004.

B **Small or Large?**
Draw a circle around the right words and then write the words.

1 A tsunami is a _____ sea wave.
           small   large

2 Some earthquakes kill _____ people.
           much   many

3 _____ earthquakes are very small.
  Most   Much

4 _____ earthquakes cause a large tsunami.
  Many   Much

Unit 07

The Food Pyramid

Reading Focus

- What is the food pyramid?
- What are some grains?
- What makes your muscles strong?

| GRAINS | VEGETABLES | FRUITS | FAT | MILK | MEAT & BEANS |

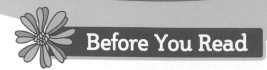

Key Words

The Five Food Groups

grains

vegetables

fruits

milk

meat and beans

energy

Food Gives Us

strong bones

strong muscles

Power Verbs

come from
Milk **comes from** cows.

include
Grains **include** rice and bread.

give energy
Food **gives energy** to your body.

keep
Milk **keeps** you healthy.

Word Families: The Five Food Groups

grains

rice, wheat, bread

vegetables

carrot, lettuce, tomato

fruits

apple, banana, strawberry

milk

milk, cheese, yogurt

meat and beans

chicken, pork, beef, fish, egg, bean

51

The Food Pyramid 14

What's your favorite food?
Do you like meat? Do you like fruits?

Foods come from plants and animals.
Grains, fruits, and vegetables come from plants.
Eggs, milk, fish, and meat come from animals.

top

MyPyramid
STEPS TO A HEALTHIER YOU
MyPyramid.gov

This is a food pyramid.
There are five food groups on the food pyramid.
They are grains, vegetables, fruits, milk,
and meat and beans.
Oils are not a food group, but you need some for good health.

bottom

Grains are foods like rice and bread.
Vegetables are foods like carrots and lettuce.
Fruits are foods like apples and bananas.
Milk includes cheese and yogurt.
Meat and beans include fish, eggs, and beans.

Grains, vegetables, and fruits give energy to your body.
Milk keeps your bones strong.
Meat and fish make your muscles strong.

▶ **Food gives us energy, strong
bones, and strong muscles.**

The food pyramid is a guide for healthy eating.
All food groups reach the top of the pyramid.
That means each kind of food is equally important.

Look at the width of each food group in the pyramid.
That shows you how much of each kind of food is best to eat.
The biggest group is grains.
That is followed by vegetables, milk, fruits, meat and beans,
and finally oils.
On the left side of the pyramid, there is a person climbing up stairs.
That shows you need to exercise every day.
This will help keep your body healthy.

Check Understanding

1 **Which food group does each picture show?**

 **a**    **b**

_____   _____

2 **Where do grains come from?**
  a plants   **b** animals   **c** milk

3 **Meat and fish make your _____ strong.**
  a energy   **b** bones   **c** muscles

• **Answer the questions below.**

1 What food groups are on the food pyramid?
  ⇨ They are _____, _____, _____, milk,
    and _____.

2 What is the food pyramid?
  ⇨ It is a guide for _____ _____.

A **Look, Read, and Write.**
Look at the pictures. Write the correct words.

| energy | grains | guide | animals |

1 ▸ Eggs and meat come from _____.

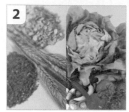

2 ▸ _____ and vegetables come from plants.

3 ▸ Food gives us _____.

4 ▸ The food pyramid is a _____ for healthy eating.

B **Grains or Vegetables?**
Draw a circle around the right words and then write the words.

1 Rice and bread are _____.
   grains   vegetables

2 Apples and bananas are _____.
   meat   fruits

3 _____ includes cheese and yogurt.
   Grain   Milk

4 Carrots are _____.
   fruits   vegetables

Unit

08

Staying Healthy

Reading Focus

- How can we stay healthy?
- How can we stay safe?

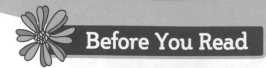

 15

Key Words

Staying Healthy

healthy foods

keeping clean

exercise

being safe outdoors

seatbelt

Keeping Safe

baby seat

helmet

following rules

Power Verbs

stay healthy
Eat healthy foods to **stay healthy**.

brush
Brush your teeth every day.

exercise
Exercise regularly.

fight
Exercise helps you **fight** diseases.

follow
Follow the rules.

wear
Wear your seatbelt in a car.

Word Families

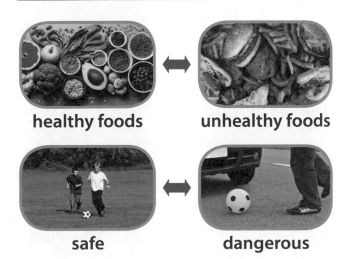

healthy foods ⟷ **unhealthy foods**

safe ⟷ **dangerous**

restroom

outdoors

Staying Healthy

16

Today, our class saw a video about healthy living.
You can do many things to stay healthy.

First, eat healthy foods.
Eating healthy foods helps you grow strong.
Eating unhealthy foods can make you sick.

▲ unhealthy foods

Second, always keep yourself clean.
Keeping clean helps you stay healthy.
Always wash your hands at these times:

- Before eating
- After using the restroom
- After playing outside

Brush your teeth at least twice a day.
Brush in the morning.
Brush before you go to bed at night.

Third, exercise regularly.
Exercise helps your body stay strong.
It also helps your body fight diseases.

Last, be safe outdoors.

We can do many things outside.

But we need to be careful.

Follow these rules when you are outdoors:

- Wear a helmet when you ride a bike.
- In a car, wear your seatbelt.
- Follow the rules when you play sports.

▲ To be safe in a car, wear your seatbelt.

Check Understanding

1 **Which activity does each picture show?**

a

b

_____   _____

2 **When should you wash your hands?**
   a before eating   b while eating
   c before using the restroom

3 **Exercise helps your body fight _____.**
   a restrooms   b diseases   c seatbelt

4 **Wear a _____ when you ride a bike.**
   a seatbelt   b helmet   c glove

- **Answer the questions below.**

1 How often should you brush your teeth?
   ⇨ You should brush your teeth at least _____ ____ _____.

2 What should you do when you play sports?
   ⇨ You should _____ _____ _____.

A **Look, Read, and Write.**
Look at the pictures. Write the correct words.

| seatbelt | unhealthy | helmet | outside |

1 _____ foods can make you sick.

2 ▸ Wash your hands after playing _____.

3 ▸ Wear a _____ when you ride a bike.

4 ▸ Wear your _____ in a car.

B **Eat or Eating?**
Draw a circle around the right words and then write the words.

1 _____ healthy foods.
   Eat   Eating

2 _____ healthy foods helps you grow strong.
   Eat   Eating

3 Always _____ yourself clean.
   keep   keeping

4 _____ clean helps you stay healthy.
   Keep   Keeping

A Look at the pictures. Write the correct words.

> cub   exercise   damage   energy

1 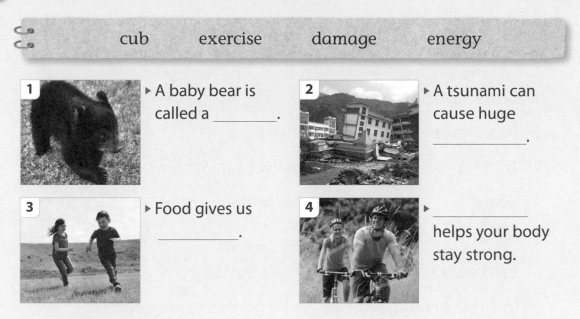 ▶ A baby bear is called a _____.

2 ▶ A tsunami can cause huge _____.

3 ▶ Food gives us _____.

4 ▶ _____ helps your body stay strong.

B Draw a circle around the right words and then write the words.

1 The giant panda lives in _____.
　　　　　　　　　　　　　　Chile   China

2 A tsunami is a _____ sea wave.
　　　　　　　small   large

3 _____ include rice and bread.
　Grains   Fats

4 _____ unhealthy foods can make you sick.
　Eat   Eating

C Complete the sentences with the words below.

| cracks | measured | claws | polar bear |
| sleep | tsunami | fur | destroy |

1 Bears have paws and sharp _____.

2 Bears have _____ on their bodies.

3 The _____ is the biggest bear in the world.

4 Bears _____ during the winter.

5 Big earthquakes can make _____ in the ground.

6 Earthquakes can _____ buildings.

7 In 2011, a huge _____ hit northeastern Japan.

8 The biggest earthquake _____ 9.5 on the Richter scale.

D Complete the sentences with the words below.

| pyramid | foods | rice | guide |
| wash | stay | rules | twice |

1 _____ come from plants and animals.

2 There are five food groups on the food _____.

3 Grains include _____ and bread.

4 The food pyramid is a _____ for healthy eating.

5 You can do many things to _____ healthy.

6 Always _____ your hands before you eat.

7 Brush your teeth at least _____ a day.

8 Follow the _____ when you play sports.

Chapter

3

Language

Mathematics

Visual Arts

Music

Unit 09

Where Is It?

Reading Focus

- Can you use some words of position?
- Where are the things in your room?

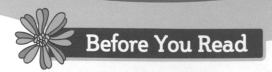
Key Words

Where Is It?

in
The pencils are **in** the pencil case.

on
The lamp is **on** the desk.

under
The dog is **under** the desk.

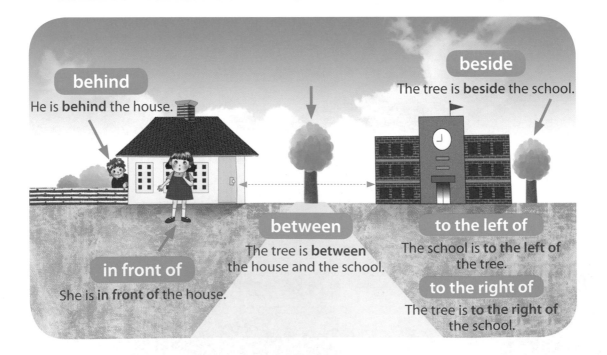

behind
He is **behind** the house.

beside
The tree is **beside** the school.

in front of
She is **in front of** the house.

between
The tree is **between** the house and the school.

to the left of
The school is **to the left of** the tree.

to the right of
The tree is **to the right of** the school.

Power Verbs

clean up
Clean up your room.

put
Put the pencils in the pencil case.

Word Families

messy ⟷ tidy = clean

Things in Mary's Room

computer

lamp

closet

desk

cell phone   pencil case

bed

bookshelf

Where Is It? 🎧 18

"Mary, your room is too messy," says her mother.

"Clean it up right now."

"Okay," answers Mary.

"I'll put the pencils in the pencil case.

And I'll put the books on the bookshelf."

Her mother says, "Your clothes are on the floor. Put them in the closet."

Mary responds, "Okay, and I will put these boxes under my bed."

"And the lamp should be on the desk," says her mother.

"Okay, Mom. How does my room look now?" Mary asks.

"It's much better," her mother answers.

Mary's room is tidy now.
The pencils are in the pencil case.
The books are on the bookshelf.
The clothes are in the closet.
The lamp is on the desk.
And the boxes are under the bed.

Do you see the cell phone?
It is beside the pencil case.
The pencil case is between the cell phone
and the lamp.

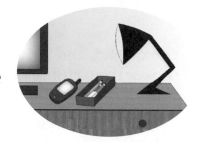

Is the closet to the left of the desk?
No, the closet is to the right of the desk.
And the bed is in front of the closet.

Check Understanding

1 Where are the books and the bed?

   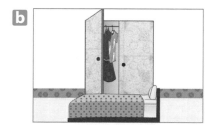

The books are _____ the bookshelf.   The bed is _____ the closet.

2 What was wrong with Mary's room?
a It was clean.   b It was small.   c It was messy.

3 Where does Mary put her lamp?
a on the desk   b in the desk   c under the desk

4 The _____ is in front of the closet.
a pencil   b bed   c chair

- **Answer the questions below.**

1 Where does Mary put her clothes?
   ⇨ She puts her clothes _____ the _____.

2 Where are the boxes? ⇨ The boxes are _____ the _____.

Vocabulary and Grammar Builder

A **Look, Read, and Write.**
Look at the pictures. Write the correct words.

> bookshelf   messy   cell phone   tidy

▸ Mary's room was too _____.

▸ Mary's room is _____ now.

▸ Mary puts the books on the _____.

▸ Mary puts the _____ beside the pencil case.

B **Beside or Between?**
Draw a circle around the right words and then write the words.

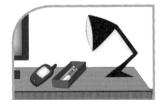   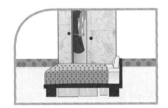

1 The cell phone is _____ the pencil case.
   beside   between

2 The pencils are _____ the pencil case.
   in   on

3 The pencil case is _____ the cell phone and the lamp.
   on   between

4 The bed is _____ the closet.
   in front of   behind

Unit 10

Addition and Subtraction

Reading Focus

- Can you add two numbers?
- Can you subtract one number from another?
- What are some symbols we use in math?

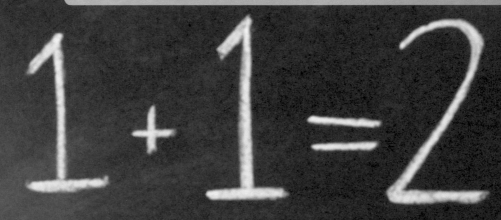

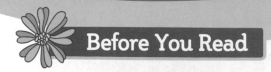
Key Words

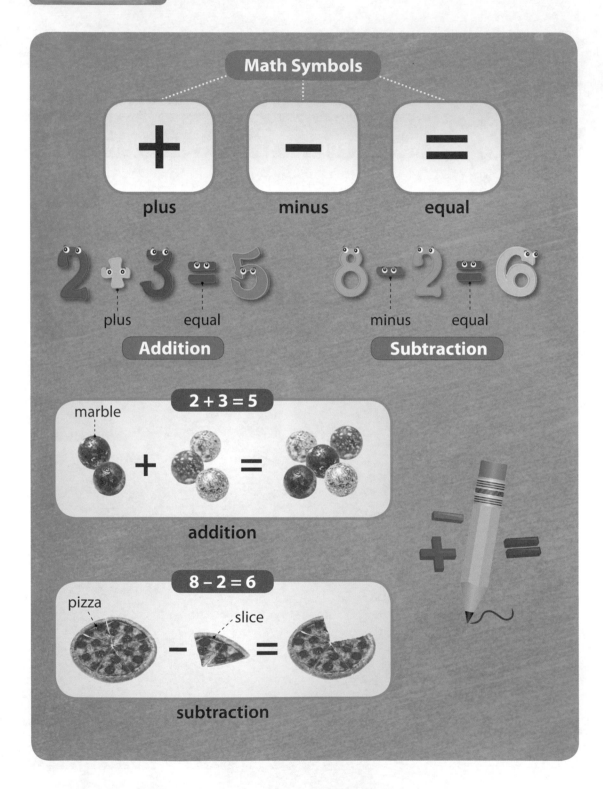

Math Symbols

+
plus

−
minus

=
equal

2 + 3 = 5
plus   equal
Addition

8 − 2 = 6
minus   equal
Subtraction

2 + 3 = 5

marble

+ =

addition

8 − 2 = 6

pizza

slice

− =

subtraction

Power Verbs

play with
He is **playing with** marbles.

put together
Let's **put** two numbers **together**.

add
Can you **add** two and three?

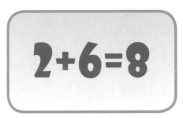

equal
Two plus six **equals** eight.

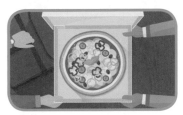

order
We **ordered** a pizza.

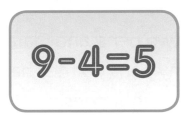

subtract
Let's **subtract** four from nine.

Word Families: Plus and Minus

2 + 1 = 3 ➡ Two **plus** one **equals** three.

5 + 6 = 11 ➡ Five **plus** six **equals** eleven.

4 − 3 = 1 ➡ Four **minus** three **equals** one.

9 − 7 = 2 ➡ Nine **minus** seven **equals** two.

Addition and Subtraction

Joe and Steve are playing with their marbles.
Joe has three marbles, and Steve has four marbles.
They put their marbles together.
How many marbles are there now?
There are seven marbles.

This is addition.
You add the two numbers 3 and 4.
We can write it like this:
$3 + 4 = 7$.
We say, "Three plus four equals seven."

▲ addition

Sue has two pens, and Clara has six pens.
How many pens do they have together?
They have eight pens.
You add the two numbers 2 and 6.
$2 + 6 = 8$.
We say, "Two plus six equals eight."

Dave orders a pizza.
It has eight slices.
Dave eats two slices.
How many slices are left?
There are six slices now.

This is subtraction.
You subtract 2 from 8.
We can write it like this:
$8 - 2 = 6$
We say, "Eight minus two equals six."

▲ subtraction

Check Understanding

1 **What does each picture show?**

a

b
$4 + 3 = 7$

_____   _____

2 **What symbol do we use to add two numbers together?**
a +   **b** −   **c** =

3 **What is four plus two?**
a two   **b** five   **c** six

4 **Eight _____ two equals six.**
a plus   **b** minus   **c** and

• **Answer the questions below.**

1 How do you say $4 + 5 = 9$?
⇨ Four _____ five _____ nine.

2 How do you say $10 - 3 = 7$?
⇨ Ten _____ three _____ seven.

Vocabulary and Grammar Builder

A **Look, Read, and Write.**
Look at the pictures. Write the correct words.

| order | subtract | add | playing |

 **1** ▸ They are _____ with marbles.

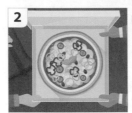 **2** ▸ Let's _____ a pizza.

 **3** ▸ Can you _____ 2 and 6?

 **4** ▸ Can you _____ 2 from 8?

B **Plus or Minus?**
Draw a circle around the right words and then write the words.

| 5+7=12 | 8−3=5 | 2+2=4 | 7−6=1 |

1 Five _____ seven equals twelve.
  plus   minus

2 Eight _____ three equals five.
  plus   minus

3 Two plus two _____ four.
  equal   equals

4 Seven minus six equals _____.
  one   two

11

Sculptures

Reading Focus

- What is a sculpture?
- What are some famous sculptures?
- Who are some famous sculptors?

Key Words

Sculptures

sculpture

statue

mobile

stone

Sculptures Are Made Of

clay

wood

metal

sculptor

artist

Power Verbs

be called
It **is called** a sculpture.

be made of
It **is made of** stone.

create
Sculptors **create** sculptures.

move
It is **moving** in the wind.

hang
Hang the mobile from the ceiling.

blow
The wind **blows**.

Word Families

as small as
It is **as small as** your thumb.

as big as
It is **as big as** the tree.

79

Sculptures

Look at these pictures.

▲ the Statue of Liberty

They are statues.
They are also called sculptures.

Sculptures are made of stone, wood, or metal.
Some sculptures are big.
One of the most famous sculptures is the Statue of Liberty.
It is a very big statue.
It is so big that people can walk inside it.

Some sculptures are small.
They can be as small as your thumb.

Do you know who makes these sculptures?
Sculptors make these sculptures.
Sculptors are artists.
They create many kinds of sculptures.

▶ Sculptors make sculptures.

Did you know that some sculptures can move?
They are called mobiles.
A mobile is a moving sculpture.
You can hang a mobile in the air.
When the wind blows, the mobile moves.

▲ A mobile is a moving
sculpture.

Check Understanding

1   What does each picture show?

   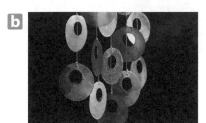

the _____ of Liberty   _____

2   What is another name for a statue?
a a sculpture   b a painting   c a mobile

3   What do sculptors make?
a paintings   b sculptures   c drawings

4   A mobile is a _____ sculpture.
a painted   b moving   c making

- **Answer the questions below.**

1   What are sculptures made of?
   ⇨ They are made of _____, _____, or _____.

2   What is a famous sculpture?
   ⇨ The _____ of _____ is a famous sculpture.

Vocabulary and Grammar Builder

A **Look, Read, and Write.**
Look at the pictures. Write the correct words.

> sculptures   sculptor   thumb   blows

1  ▸ A _____ is an artist.

2 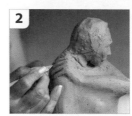 ▸ Sculptors create _____.

3  ▸ Some sculptures are as small as your _____.

4  ▸ A mobile moves when the wind _____.

B **Call or Called?**
Draw a circle around the right words and then write the words.

1 Statues are also _____ sculptures.
        call   called

2 Sculptures are _____ of stone, wood, or metal.
        make   made

3 Mobiles are _____ sculptures.
        moving   moved

4 You can _____ a mobile in the air.
        hang   hanging

Unit 12

A World of Instruments

Reading Focus

- What are some traditional musical instruments?
- How do these musical instruments sound?

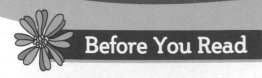

Key Words

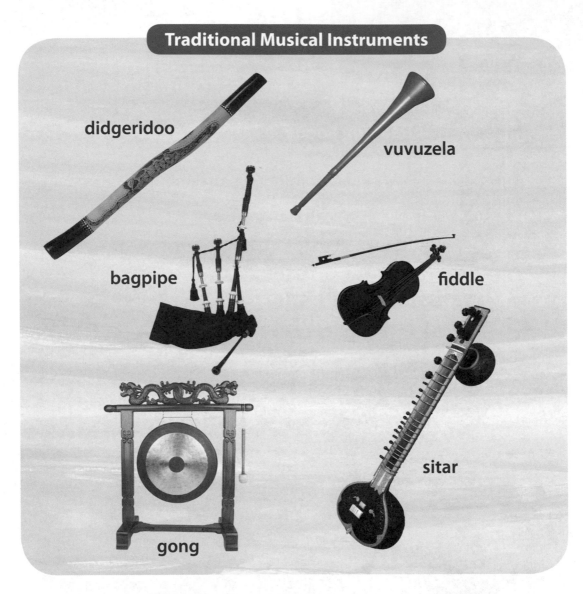

Traditional Musical Instruments

didgeridoo

vuvuzela

bagpipe

fiddle

gong

sitar

folk music

Power Verbs

play
People **play** musical instruments.

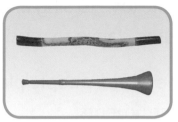

be similar to
It **is similar to** the didgeridoo.

make a sound
It **makes a sound** like an elephant.

sound like
The bagpipe **sounds like** a horn.

be like
A fiddle **is like** a violin.

be used for
The sitar **is used for** classical music.

Word Families: Three Groups of Music Instruments

wind instrument	horn · didgeridoo · vuvuzela
string instrument	violin · fiddle · sitar
percussion instrument	drum · gong

A World of Instruments

Many people love to sing and dance.
They sing and dance to music.

Around the world, people play many different
musical instruments.
Let's look at some of them.

▲ didgeridoo

In Australia, some people play the didgeridoo.
This is a long, thin wind instrument.
It makes a buzzing sound.

In South Africa, some people play the vuvuzela.
It is similar to the didgeridoo.
It makes a sound like an elephant.

▲ vuvuzela

In Scotland, some people play the bagpipe.
It sounds like a horn.

In the United States, some people play the fiddle.
It is like the violin.
But people play folk music on a fiddle.

▶ bagpipe

▲ fiddle

In Asia, some people play the gong.
It is a percussion instrument.
There are many kinds of gongs.

In India, some people play the sitar.
It is a string instrument.
It is used for Indian classical music.

▲ gong

▲ sitar

Check Understanding

1 **Which musical instrument does each picture show?**

a

b

_____   _____

2 **Where do people play the didgeridoo?**
   a in Scotland   **b** in India   **c** in Australia

3 **What kind of instrument is the gong?**
   a a string instrument   **b** a percussion instrument
   c a wind instrument

4 **The _____ is used for Indian classical music.**
   a gong   **b** vuvuzela   **c** sitar

- **Answer the questions below.**

1 What does the vuvuzela sound like?   ⇨ It sounds like an _____.

2 What kind of music do people play on the fiddle?
   ⇨ They play _____ _____.

Vocabulary and Grammar Builder

A **Look, Read, and Write.**
Look at the pictures. Write the correct words.

| like | buzzing | Scotland | similar |

1 ▸ The bagpipe is played in _____.

2 ▸ The vuvuzela is _____ to the didgeridoo.

3 ▸ A fiddle is _____ a violin.

4 ▸ The didgeridoo makes a _____ sound.

B **What Do They Play?**
Draw a circle around the right words and then write the words.

1 The _____ is played in Australia.
    vuvuzela   didgeridoo

2 The _____ is played in South Africa.
    vuvuzela   didgeridoo

3 The _____ is played in the United States.
    sitar   fiddle

4 The _____ is played in Asia.
    gong   bagpipe

A Look at the pictures. Write the correct words.

| subtract | sculptures | messy | folk music |

1 ▸ Mary's room was too _____.

2 ▸ Can you _____ 2 from 8?

3 ▸ Sculptors create _____.

4 ▸ People play _____ on a fiddle.

B Draw a circle around the right words and then write the words.

1 The cell phone is _____ the pencil case.
    beside   between

2 Five _____ eight equals thirteen.
    plus   minus

3 Mobiles are _____ sculptures.
    moving   moved

4 The didgeridoo is _____ in Australia.
    playing   played

C Complete the sentences with the words below.

add	between	in	tidy
minus	equals	subtract	on

1 Your clothes are _____ the floor.

2 Put your clothes _____ the closet.

3 The pencil case is _____ the cell phone and the lamp.

4 Mary cleaned up her room. It is _____ now.

5 We say, "Three plus four _____ seven." $(3 + 4 = 7)$

6 You _____ the two numbers 2 and 6. $(2 + 6 = 8)$

7 You _____ 2 from 8. $(8 - 2 = 6)$

8 We say, "Eight _____ two equals six."

D Complete the sentences with the words below.

made	thumb	elephant	statues
mobile	didgeridoo	percussion	sitar

1 _____ are also called sculptures.

2 Sculptures are _____ of stone, wood, or metal.

3 Some sculptures can be as small as your _____.

4 You can hang a _____ in the air.

5 In Australia, some people play the _____.

6 The vuvuzela makes a sound like an _____.

7 The gong is a _____ instrument.

8 The _____ is used for Indian classical music.

Word List

Word List

01 Countries in the World
世界各國

1	**country**	國家 * 複數：countries
2	**in the world**	世界上
3	**how many**	多少……
4	**some**	有些
5	**Russia**	俄國
6	**the biggest**	最大的
7	**the first**	第一 (= the 1st)
8	**Canada**	加拿大
9	**the second**	第二 (= the 2nd)
10	**the United States**	美國
11	**the third**	第三 (= the 3rd)
12	**China**	中國
13	**Brazil**	巴西
14	**the fourth**	第四 (= the 4th)
15	**the fifth**	第五 (= the 5th)
16	**the smallest**	最小的
17	**Vatican City**	梵蒂岡市
18	**be located**	位於……
19	**inside**	在……裡面
20	**Rome**	羅馬
21	**Italy**	義大利
22	**bigger than**	比……大
23	**city block**	城區
24	**tiny**	很小的
25	**population**	人口
26	**only**	只有……
27	**about**	大約
28	**live in**	住在……
29	**billion**	十億
30	**1.39 billion**	13.9億 (=1,390,000,000)
31	**India**	印度
32	**more than**	比……多

33	**1.3 billion**	13億 (＝1,300,000,000)
34	**million**	百萬
35	**300 million**	3億 (＝300,000,000)
36	**every country**	每個國家
37	**its own**	自己的……
38	**flag**	旗子
39	**national flag**	國旗
40	**national anthem**	國歌
41	**follow**	遵守
42	**the same**	相同的
43	**law**	法律
44	**language**	語言
45	**culture**	文化

02 The World's Best
世界之最

1	**the best**	最…… （好、高、大等）
2	**around the world**	世界各地
3	**some**	有些
4	**low**	低的
5	**others**	其他的
6	**high**	高的
7	**Mount Everest**	聖母峰
8	**the world's tallest**	全世界最高的
9	**rise**	高聳；高出
10	**be located**	位於……
11	**the Himalayas**	喜馬拉雅山脈
12	**border**	邊界
13	**Nepal**	尼泊爾

14	**call**	稱……為……
15	**top**	頂端
16	**the Andes (Mountains)**	安地斯山脈
17	**the world's longest**	全世界最長的
18	**mountain range**	山脈
19	**stretch**	延續；連綿
20	**South America**	南美洲
21	**Europe**	歐洲
22	**the Alps**	阿爾卑斯山脈
23	**Mont Blanc**	白朗峰
24	**the highest**	最高的
25	**peak**	山峰
26	**the Nile River**	尼羅河
27	**Africa**	非洲
28	**flow into**	流進……
29	**the Mediterranean Sea**	地中海
30	**the Amazon River**	亞馬遜河
31	**another**	另一個
32	**huge**	巨大的
33	**across**	橫越；穿過
34	**the Atlantic Ocean**	大西洋
35	**the world's largest**	全世界最大的
36	**desert**	沙漠
37	**the Sahara (Desert)**	撒哈拉（沙漠）
38	**the Arabian Desert**	阿拉伯沙漠
39	**the Middle East**	中東
40	**the Gobi Desert**	戈壁沙漠
41	**the world's highest**	全世界最高的
42	**waterfall**	瀑布

43	Angel Falls	天使瀑布
44	fall	降下；掉落
45	Venezuela	委內瑞拉

Earth Is Our Home
地球是我們的家

1	earth	地球
2	look at	看
3	picture	圖片
4	use	使用
5	need	需要
6	live	生存；生活
7	drink	喝
8	grow	生長；成長
9	food	食物
10	wash clothes	洗衣服
11	cook food	煮食物
12	plant	植物
13	also	也……
14	animal	動物
15	too	也……
16	without	沒有……
17	living thing	生物
18	air	空氣
19	breathe	呼吸
20	clean	乾淨的
21	need to	需要……
22	keep	保持
23	natural resources	天然資源

24	nature	大自然
25	land	土地
26	important	重要的
27	fruit	水果；果實
28	every day	每天
29	should not	不該
30	waste	浪費
31	save	節約
32	disappear	消失

Recycle, Reuse, and Reduce
回收、再利用、減量

1	recycle	回收
2	reuse	再利用
3	reduce	減少；減量
4	our class	我們的班級
5	learn	學習
6	be learning	正在學
7	how to	如何……
8	save	拯救；節約；儲存
9	less	少的
10	trash	垃圾
11	first	首先
12	collect	收集
13	every Monday	每個禮拜一
14	what	（關係代名詞）
15	what our class collects 我們班收集的東西	
16	paper	紙；紙張

17	can	罐頭	
18	plastic	塑膠	
19	glass	玻璃	
20	then	接著;然後	
21	put into	放進……	
22	recycling bin	回收箱	
23	be made into	製作成……	
24	new things	新的東西	
25	again and again	一次又一次	
26	both sides	兩面都……	
27	bag	袋子;紙袋	
28	box	箱子;紙箱	
29	what we use	我們所使用的	
30	brush one's teeth	刷牙	
31	turn off	關掉;關上	
32	leave a room	離開房間	
33	light	燈	

05 A World of Animals: Bears
動物世界:熊

1	bear	熊
2	fur	(獸類的)毛皮
3	body	身體 *複數:bodies
4	black	黑色
5	brown	棕色
6	white	白色
7	paw	腳爪;腳掌
8	sharp	鋒利的

9	claw	爪子
10	baby bear	小熊;熊寶寶
11	be called	被稱為……
12	cub	(熊、獅、虎等的)幼獸
13	tiny	很小的
14	be born	出生
15	drink milk	喝奶
16	grow up	成長;長大
17	leave	離開
18	den	洞穴
19	hunt fish	抓魚
20	polar bear	北極熊
21	the North Pole	北極
22	sun bear	馬來熊
23	rainforest	雨林
24	giant panda	貓熊
25	brown bear	棕熊
26	many parts of the world	世界上很多地方
27	grizzly bear	灰棕熊
28	North America	北美洲
29	late fall	晚秋
30	find	尋找
31	winter home	冬天的家;度冬棲地
32	sleep	睡覺
33	during the winter	冬天時
34	move	移動

06 Earthquakes
地震

1	earthquake	地震
2	rumble	隆隆響
3	ground	地面
4	shake	搖晃
5	happen	發生
6	most	大部分
7	feel	感覺
8	crack	裂縫；裂痕
9	make cracks	造成裂縫
10	destroy	摧毀
11	kill	扼殺；殺害
12	under	在……下面
13	ocean floor	海底；海床
14	cause	造成
15	sea wave	海浪
16	tsunami	海嘯
17	damage	損害；損失
18	hit	襲擊；打擊
19	northeastern	東北邊；東北部
20	Japan	日本
21	thousands of	數以千計的
22	Indonesia	印尼
23	200,000 people	20萬人
24	Chile	智利
25	measure	測量
26	on the Richter scale	芮式規模

07 The Food Pyramid
食物金字塔

1	food pyramid	食物金字塔
2	favorite food	喜愛的食物
3	meat	肉類
4	come from	出自於…
5	grain	穀物
6	fruit	水果
7	vegetables	蔬菜類
8	egg	雞蛋
9	milk	奶類
10	fish	魚肉
11	five food groups	五大類食物
12	oils	油類
13	only	只要
14	amount	量
15	in small amounts	少量的
16	like	例如；就像是……
17	rice	米飯
18	bread	麵包
19	carrot	胡蘿蔔
20	lettuce	萵苣
21	include	包括；包含
22	cheese	起司；乳酪
23	yogurt	優格
24	bean	豆類
25	give energy	給予能量
26	keep	保持
27	bone	骨骼
28	muscle	肌肉

29	guide	指標
30	healthy	健康的
31	reach	抵達；延伸到
32	top	頂端
33	width	寬度
34	finally	最後
35	climb	攀爬
36	stair	樓梯
37	exercise	運動

08 Staying Healthy
永保健康

1	stay	保持；留住
2	healthy	健康的
3	stay healthy	保持健康
4	healthy living	健康生活
5	healthy foods	健康的食物
6	unhealthy foods	不健康的食物
7	sick	生病
8	keep oneself clean	保持……自己的乾淨
9	wash one's hands	洗手
10	at these times	在這些時間點
11	restroom	廁所
12	play outside	在戶外玩
13	brush one's teeth	刷牙
14	at least	至少
15	twice a day	一天兩次
16	go to bed	上床睡覺
17	exercise	運動

18	regularly	規律地
19	fight diseases	對抗疾病
20	last	最後
21	outdoors	戶外
22	careful	小心
23	follow	遵守
24	rule	規則
25	wear a helmet	戴安全帽
26	ride a bike	騎腳踏車
27	wear one's seatbelt	繫安全帶
28	play sports	運動

09 Where Is It?
在哪兒呢？

1	room	房間
2	too	太……
3	messy	髒亂；混亂
4	clean up	整理；清理
5	right now	現在馬上
6	put	放（進）
7	pencil	鉛筆
8	in	在……裡面
9	pencil case	鉛筆盒
10	on	在……上面
11	bookshelf	書櫃
12	clothes	衣服
13	floor	地板
14	closet	衣櫥
15	respond	回答
16	under	在……下面
17	bed	床

18	lamp	燈
19	should be	應該是……
20	How does…look?	……看起來如何？
21	much better	好多了
22	tidy	整齊的；整潔的
23	cell phone	手機 (= mobile phone)
24	beside	在……旁邊
25	between	在……之間
26	to the left of	在……左邊
27	to the right of	在……右邊
28	in front of	在……前面

10 Addition and Subtraction
加法和減法

1	addition	加法
2	subtraction	減法
3	play with	玩……
4	marble	彈珠
5	put…together	將……放在一起
6	add	加；加上
7	like this	像這樣
8	plus	加；加上
9	equal	等於
10	order	訂……；點餐
11	pizza	披薩
12	slice	薄片；片
13	be left	剩下
14	subtract	減；減掉
15	minus	減；減掉

11 Sculptures
雕塑藝術

1	sculpture	雕塑品
2	look at	看
3	statue	雕像
4	be called	被稱為……
5	be made of	由……所製作
6	stone	石頭
7	wood	木頭
8	metal	金屬
9	famous	有名的
10	the Statue of Liberty	自由女神像
11	so…that…	如此……以致於……
12	inside	在裡面
13	as small as	像……一樣小
14	thumb	拇指
15	sculptor	雕刻家
16	artist	藝術家
17	create	創作
18	many kinds of	很多種類
19	move	移動
20	mobile	平衡吊掛雕塑
21	moving sculpture	動態雕塑品
22	hang	把……掛起；掛
23	in the air	在半空中
24	blow	（風）吹；吹動

12 A World of Instruments
樂器的世界

1	instrument	樂器
2	play	演奏
3	different	不同的
4	musical instrument	樂器
5	Australia	澳洲
6	didgeridoo	迪吉里杜管（澳洲土著使用的一種樂器）
7	thin	細的
8	wind instrument	管樂器
9	make a sound	製造聲響
10	buzzing sound	嗡嗡聲
11	South Africa	南非
12	vuvuzela	嗚嗚茲拉（一種南非足球迷在加油時使用的長形喇叭狀樂器，能發出巨大的聲響）
13	be similar to	與……類似
14	elephant	大象
15	Scotland	蘇格蘭
16	bagpipe	風笛
17	sound like	聽起來像……
18	horn	號角；小號
19	the United States	美國
20	fiddle	提琴
21	be like	跟……很像
22	violin	小提琴
23	folk music	民俗音樂
24	Asia	亞洲
25	gong	銅鑼
26	percussion instrument	打擊樂器
27	India	印度
28	sitar	西塔琴（形似吉他的印度弦樂器）
29	string instrument	絃樂器
30	be used for	被用於……
31	Indian classical music	印度傳統音樂

Answers and Translations

Reading Focus 閱讀焦點

- What are some big countries? 有哪些大國？
- What are some small countries? 有哪些小國？
- Which countries have many people? 哪些國家有很多人口？

Key Words 關鍵字彙

The World's Biggest Countries
世界上最大的國家

the 1st
the first
第一名

the 2nd
the second
第二名

Russia
俄羅斯

Canada
加拿大

the 3rd
the third
第三名

the 4th
the fourth
第四名

the 5th
the fifth
第五名

the United States
美國

China
中國

Brazil
巴西

The World's Smallest Countries
世界上最小的國家

the 1st
the first
第一名

the 2nd
the second
第二名

Vatican City
梵蒂岡市

Monaco
摩納哥

Power Verbs 核心動詞

be located	**live in**	**follow**
位於……	住在……	遵守
Vatican City **is located** in Rome.	1.39 billion people **live in** China.	You should **follow** the law.
梵蒂岡市位於羅馬。	有 13.9 億人口住在中國。	你應該要遵守法律。

Word Families: Words for Countries
相關字彙：關於國家的用詞

population
人口

100	**hundred** 百
1,000	**thousand** 千
1,000,000	**million** 百萬
1,000,000,000	**billion** 十億

(national) flag
（國）旗

national anthem
國歌

law
法律

country
國家

culture
文化

language
語言

Countries in the World 世界各國

世界上有多少國家？
全世界有 193 個國家。

有些國家大；有些國家小，
俄國是世界上最大的國家，
加拿大是世界排名第二大的國家，
美國是世界排名第三大的國家，
中國和巴西分別是世界上第四大和第五大的國家。

那世界上最小的國家是哪裡呢？
就是梵蒂岡市，
它位於義大利的羅馬。
它比一個城區還要小，
也只有非常少量的人口，
梵蒂岡市的人口大約只有一千人。

哪一個國家擁有最多的人口？
中國是全世界擁有最多人口的國家，
大約有 13.9 億人口。
印度則有 13 億多的人口，
而美國有 3 億多的人口。

每個國家都有自己的國旗，
也有自己的國歌。
人們在國家裡要遵守一樣的法律，
大家說相同的語言，
也擁有共同的文化。

Check Understanding 文意測驗

1 下列圖片中分別是哪一個國家？

a **China** 中國　　　b **Vatican City** 梵蒂岡市

2 世界上最大的是哪個國家？ **c**

a 加拿大　　　b 中國　　　c 俄羅斯

3 世界上最小的是哪個國家？ **b**

a 羅馬　　　b 梵蒂岡　　　c 巴西

4 哪一個國家擁有世界上最多的人口？ **b**

a 美國　　　b 中國　　　c 印度

● 回答問題

1 What are the five biggest countries in the world? 世界上最大的國家是哪五個？
⇨ They are <u>Russia</u>, <u>Canada</u>, the <u>United States</u>, China, and <u>Brazil</u>.
分別是俄國、加拿大、美國、中國和巴西。

2 What is the smallest country in the world? 世界上最小的國家是哪一個？
⇨ <u>Vatican City</u> is the <u>smallest</u> country in the world. 梵蒂岡市是世界上最小的國家。

Vocabulary and Grammar Builder 字彙與文法練習

Ⓐ 看圖填空：依照圖片選出正確的單字。

1 There are 193 <u>countries</u> in the world. 全世界有 193 個國家。

2 Vatican City is <u>located</u> inside Rome. 梵蒂岡市位於羅馬。

3 About 1.39 <u>billion</u> people live in China. 中國大約有 13.9 億人口。

4 Every country has its own <u>flag</u>. 每個國家都有自己的國旗。

Ⓑ 序數：圈出正確的單字，並填入空格中。

1 Canada is the _____second_____ biggest country in the world. 加拿大是世界上排名第二大的國家。
first (second)

2 The United States is the _____third_____ biggest country in the world. 美國是世界上排名第三大的國家。
second (third)

3 China is the _____fourth_____ biggest country in the world. 中國是世界上排名第四大的國家。
(fourth) fifth

4 Brazil is the _____fifth_____ biggest country in the world. 巴西是世界上排名第五大的國家。
fourth (fifth)

Unit 02

The World's Best
世界之最

Reading Focus 閱讀焦點

- What is the world's tallest mountain? 世界上最高的山是哪一座？
- What is the world's longest river? 世界上最長的河是哪一條？
- What is the world's largest desert? 世界上最大的沙漠是哪裡？

Key Words 關鍵字彙

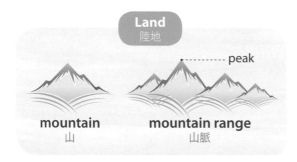

Land
陸地

peak

mountain
山

mountain range
山脈

Water
水

the Nile River
尼羅河

the Amazon River
亞馬遜河

the Mediterranean Sea
地中海

waterfall
瀑布

Desert
沙漠

the Sahara Desert
撒哈拉沙漠

the Arabian Desert
阿拉伯沙漠

the Gobi Desert
戈壁沙漠

Power Verbs 核心動詞

rise
高聳；高出

That mountain **rises** high.
山峰高聳。

the Andes

stretch
綿延；連續

The Andes **stretch** very long.
安地斯山脈綿延很長的距離。

flow
（河水等）流動

The river **flows** to the sea.
河流往大海流去。

fall
落下；下垂

The waterfall **falls** 807m.
這個瀑布高度 807 公尺。

Word Families 相關字彙

some
有些

others
其他

Some are low.
有些很低。

Others are high.
其他很高。

one
其中之一

another
另一個

The Sahara is **one** huge desert.
撒哈拉沙漠是一片非常大的沙漠。

The Gobi is **another** huge desert.
戈壁沙漠是另一片很大的沙漠。

the Himalayas
喜馬拉雅山脈

the Andes
安地斯山脈

Mountain Ranges
山脈

the Alps
阿爾卑斯山脈

the Rockies
洛磯山脈

The World's Best 世界之最

世界各地有許多山峰，
有些低、有些高。

聖母峰是世界最高的山峰，
它有 8,850 公尺高，
位於尼泊爾與中國交界處的喜馬拉雅山脈，
人們稱它為「世界的屋頂」。

安地斯山脈是世界上最長的山脈，
它連綿了 7,000 公里，
座落於南美洲。

在歐洲，有座阿爾卑斯山脈，
而其中最高的山峰是白朗峰。

世界最長的河流是尼羅河，
位於非洲，
流進地中海。
亞馬遜河是另一條大河，
位於南美洲，
橫越巴西，最後流進大西洋。

世界上最大的沙漠是位於非洲的撒哈拉沙漠，
接著是中東的阿拉伯沙漠，
亞洲的戈壁沙漠也是另一個廣大的沙漠。

世界最高的瀑布是天使瀑布，
它從 807 公尺急沖而下，
位於南美洲的委內瑞拉。

Check Understanding 文意測驗

1 下列圖片中分別是什麼？
   a **mountain range** 山脈　　b **waterfall** 瀑布

2 哪一座山峰被稱為「世界的屋頂」？ **a**
   a 聖母峰　　b 白朗峰　　c 安地斯山脈

3 阿爾卑斯山脈最高的山峰是？ **b**
   a 安地斯山脈　　b 白朗峰　　c 喜馬拉雅山脈

4 世界上最大的沙漠是_____。 **b**
   a 戈壁沙漠　　b 撒哈拉沙漠　　c 阿拉伯沙漠

● 回答問題

1 Where are the Andes Mountains? 安地斯山脈在哪裡？
   ⇨ They are in **South** **America**. 它位於南美洲。

2 What is the world's highest waterfall? 世界最高的瀑布是哪一個？
   ⇨ It is **Angel** **Falls** in **Venezuela**, South America. 就是位於南美洲委內瑞拉的天使瀑布。

Vocabulary and Grammar Builder 字彙與文法練習

Ⓐ 看圖填空：依照圖片選出正確的單字。
   1 Mount Everest is in the **Himalayas**. 聖母峰屬於喜馬拉雅山脈。
   2 The Himalayas are on the **border** of Nepal and China. 喜馬拉雅山脈座落於尼泊爾與中國的交界處。
   3 Mont Blanc is the highest **peak** in the Alps. 白朗峰是阿爾卑斯山脈的最高峰。
   4 The Amazon River is another **huge** river. 亞馬遜河是另一條大河。

Ⓑ 單字選填：圈出正確的單字，並填入空格中。
   1 Mount Everest ___**rises**___ high. 聖母峰高聳入雲。
      (rises) stretches
   2 The Andes Mountains ___**stretch**___ very long. 安地斯山脈綿延很長的距離。
      rise (stretch)
   3 The Nile River ___**flows**___ into the Mediterranean Sea. 尼羅河流進地中海。
      falls (flows)
   4 Angel Falls ___**falls**___ 807m. 天使瀑布高 807 公尺。
      (falls) flows

105

Unit 03 Earth Is Our Home

地球是我們的家

Reading Focus 閱讀焦點

- What do we need to live? 我們需要什麼才能生存？
- What are some natural resources? 有哪些天然資源？
- How do we use natural resources? 我們如何使用天然資源？

Key Words 關鍵字彙

Natural Resources
天然資源

water
水

air
空氣

land
土地

tree
樹

oil
油；石油

coal
煤

fruits
水果

Things from Trees
樹的產品

paper
紙張

furniture
家具

house
房子

Power Verbs 核心動詞

need
需要
We **need** water to live.
我們需要水才能生存。

use
使用
We **use** water every day.
我們天天都要用水。

wash
洗
We **wash** clothes.
我們洗衣服。

cook
煮；料理
We **cook** food.
我們料理食物。

breathe
呼吸
We **breathe** air.
我們呼吸空氣。

disappear
消失
The trees will **disappear**.
樹木會消失。

Word Families 相關字彙

living things
生物

people
人類

plants
植物

animals
動物

clean
乾淨的

The water is **clean**.
這水很乾淨。

dirty
髒的

The water is **dirty**.
這水很髒。

waste
浪費

Don't **waste** water.
不要浪費水。

save
節約

Save water.
節約用水。

106

Earth Is Our Home 地球是我們的家

看看這些圖片，
他們如何使用水？

我們需要水才能生存，
我們要喝水，
我們要為植物澆水，
我們需要水來洗衣服，還有料理食物。

植物也要靠水才能成長，
動物也需要水才能生存，
沒有了水，所有的生物都無法存活。

我們要呼吸空氣，
當水與空氣不再乾淨，我們就無法取用，
所以我們必須保持水和空氣的乾淨。

水和空氣是天然資源，
天然資源來自大自然，
空氣、水和土地都是重要的天然資源。

樹木是另一種天然資源，
我們可以利用樹木做很多東西，
也可以吃樹上結的水果。

地球是我們的家，
我們每天都在使用天然資源，
所以我們不應該浪費這些資源，
如果我們不珍惜這些天然資源，它們便會消失。

Check Understanding 文意測驗

1 下列圖片中是何種天然資源？
   a **land / soil** 土地 / 泥土   **b** **tree** 樹木

2 洗衣服需要什麼？ **b**
   a 土地   **b** 水   **c** 空氣

3 天然資源從哪裡來？ **c**
   a 外太空   **b** 天空   **c** 大自然

4 我們不該_____天然資源。 **c**
   a 使用   **b** 節約   **c** 浪費

● 回答問題

1 What natural resources should we keep clean? 我們應該保持什麼天然資源乾淨？
   ⇨ We should keep the **water** and **air** clean. 我們應該保持水和空氣乾淨。

2 What will happen if we do not save our natural resources? 如果我們浪費天然資源，會發生什麼事？
   ⇨ They will **disappear**. 它們會消失。

Vocabulary and Grammar Builder 字彙與文法練習

Ⓐ 看圖填空：依照圖片選出正確的單字。

1 Living things **need** water to live. 生物需要水才能生存。

2 Water and land are **natural resources**. 水和土地都是天然資源。

3 We need to keep the water **clean**. 我們必須保持水的乾淨。

4 We should **save** our natural resources. 我們應該珍惜天然資源。

Ⓑ 單字選填：圈出正確的單字，並填入空格中。

1 We ___**drink**___ water. 我們要喝水。
   (drink) wash

2 People ___**breathe**___ air. 人們呼吸空氣。
   drink (breathe)

3 People ___**wash**___ clothes with water. 人們用水洗衣服。
   (wash) make

4 People should not ___**waste**___ resources. 人們不應該浪費資源。
   save (waste)

107

Recycle, Reuse, and Reduce

回收、再利用、減量

Reading Focus 閱讀焦點

• What things can you recycle? 哪些東西可以回收？
• What things can you use again? 哪些東西可以重複使用？
• What things can you use less of? 哪些東西可以減少使用？

Key Words 關鍵字彙

paper
紙張

can
罐頭

We Recycle!
回收！

plastic
塑膠

glass
玻璃

bottle
瓶子

Paper
紙張

newspaper
報紙

magazine
雜誌

bag
紙袋

box
紙箱

Power Verbs 核心動詞

recycle
回收
Recycle cans.
回收罐頭。

reuse
再利用
Reuse boxes.
紙箱重複使用。

reduce
減少；降低
Reduce! Use less paper.
減量！紙用少一點。

collect
收集
We **collect** paper every week.
我們每個禮拜都會收集紙張。

put into
放進
Put the glass **into** the recycling bin.
把玻璃放進回收箱。

turn off
關上（水龍頭等）
Turn off the water.
把水關上。

Word Families 相關字彙

trash
垃圾
➡

trash can
垃圾桶

recycling things
回收物
➡

recycling bin
回收箱

less
少的
⬌

more
多的

Recycle, Reuse, and Reduce 回收、再利用、減量

我是蘇珊，
我們班正在學習如何拯救天然資源，
我們可以回收、再利用、減量。
這樣可以減少垃圾，
也可以幫助節約天然資源。

首先，我們回收很多東西。
我們班每個星期一都會收集東西來回收，
這裡就是我們收集的東西，
我們收集紙張，
我們收集罐頭，
我們收集塑膠，
我們收集玻璃。

接著，將它們放進回收箱，
這些東西可以用來製作新的東西，
然後我們就可以一次又一次地使用它們。

我們也能重複使用紙張，
可以使用紙張的背面。
我們存放紙袋和紙箱，
然後重複利用它們。

我們也可以減少使用量，
當你刷牙的時候，把水關上。
當你離開房間的時候，關掉電燈。

Check Understanding 文意測驗

1 下列圖片中分別是哪一種回收物？
   a cans 罐頭   **b** paper 紙張

2 回收有什麼幫助？ **a**
   a 減少垃圾。   **b** 製造更多的垃圾。   **c** 減少罐頭。

3 我們能如何重複利用紙張？ **b**
   a 使用紙張的一面   **b** 使用紙張的兩面   **c** 不要使用它

4 當你刷牙的時候，把水_____。 **a**
   a 關掉   **b** 進去   **c** 打開

● 回答問題

1 What things can we collect? 我們可以收集些什麼來回收？
   ⇨ We can collect **paper**, **cans**, **plastic**, and **glass**. 我們可以收集紙張、罐頭、塑膠和玻璃。

2 What should we do when we leave a room? 當我們離開房間的時候，應該做些什麼？
   ⇨ We should **turn** off the **light**. 我們應該關掉電燈。

Vocabulary and Grammar Builder 字彙與文法練習

A 看圖填空：依照圖片選出正確的單字。

1 We **collect** paper every week. 我們每個禮拜都收集紙張。

2 We can **recycle** many things. 我們可以回收很多東西。

3 We **put** them into the recycling bin. 我們將它們放進回收箱。

4 When you brush your teeth, **turn off** the water. 當你刷牙的時候，把水關上。

B 單字選填： 圈出正確的單字，並填入空格中。

1 Recycling makes ___**less**___ trash. 回收可以減少垃圾。
   (less) more

2 We can save bags and boxes to ___**reuse**___ them. 我們可以存放袋子和箱子來重複使用它們。
   (reuse) reduce

3 We can also ___**reduce**___ what we use. 我們也可以減少使用量。
   (reduce) waste

4 When you leave a room, turn ___**off**___ the lights. 當你離開房間的時候，關掉電燈。
   on (off)

A World of Animals: Bears

動物世界：熊

Reading Focus　閱讀焦點

• What does a bear look like?　熊的外觀是長什麼樣子？

• What are some kinds of bears?　熊有哪些種類？

• Where do bears live?　熊住在哪裡？

Key Words 關鍵字彙

Bears
熊

polar bear
北極熊

giant panda
熊貓

brown bear
棕熊

black bear
黑熊

grizzly bear
灰棕熊

sun bear
馬來熊

A Bear's Body Parts
熊的身體部位

ears
耳朵

eyes
眼睛

snout
鼻子；口鼻部

paw
腳掌

fur
毛皮

claw
（動物的）爪

Power Verbs 核心動詞

be called
被稱為……

A baby bear **is called** a cub.
小熊被稱為幼熊。

drink milk
喝奶

Cubs **drink milk** from their mothers.
幼熊喝媽媽的奶。

grow up
成長；長大

Bears leave home when they **grow up**.
熊長大後會離開家。

find
尋找

Bears **find** winter homes.
熊尋找冬天的家。

sleep
睡覺

Bears **sleep** in the winter.
熊冬天時都在睡覺。

move
移動

Bears do not **move** during the winter.
熊整個冬天都不會動。

Word Families: The Places Bears Live 相關字彙：熊住的地方

rainforest
雨林

North Pole
北極

Places Bears Live
熊住的地方

forest
森林

cave
洞窟

den
洞穴

Bears 熊

看看這些熊，
牠們身上覆蓋著毛皮，
有黑色、棕色和白色。
熊有腳掌和鋒利的爪子。

小熊被稱為幼熊，
幼熊剛出生時非常小，
牠們喝媽媽的奶。
當幼熊長大，牠們就會離開媽媽。

熊住在洞穴裡，
牠們會吃各種食物，
有些熊甚至會抓魚。

北極熊是世界上最大的熊，
住在北極圈附近。
馬來熊是世界上最小的熊，
住在雨林。

熊貓住在中國，
牠有黑白相間的毛皮。

棕熊則在世界上很多地方都能看到牠的蹤跡，
而灰棕熊住在北美洲。

在晚秋的時候，很多熊都會開始尋找冬天的家，
牠們整個冬天都在睡覺，
牠們整個冬天不吃不喝，也不會動。

Check Understanding 文意測驗

1 下列圖片中分別是什麼種類的熊？
   a <u>giant panda</u> 熊貓　　　　　　**b** <u>polar bear</u> 北極熊

2 熊的身上有什麼？ **c**
   a 羽毛　　　　　**b** 鱗片　　　　　**c** 毛皮

3 世界上最大的熊是什麼熊？ **a**
   a 北極熊　　　　　**b** 馬來熊　　　　　**c** 棕熊

4 _____是熊的家。 **b**
   a 幼熊　　　　　**b** 洞穴　　　　　**c** 腳爪

● 回答問題

1 Where does the giant panda live? 熊貓住在哪裡？
   ⇨ The giant panda <u>lives</u> in <u>China</u>. 熊貓住在中國。

2 What do bears do in the winter? 熊冬天都做些什麼？
   ⇨ They <u>sleep</u> during the winter. 牠們冬天都在睡覺。

Vocabulary and Grammar Builder 字彙與文法練習

A 看圖填空：依照圖片選出正確的單字。

1 Bears have sharp <u>claws</u> on their paws. 熊的腳掌上有鋒利的爪子。

2 A baby bear is called a <u>cub</u>. 小熊被稱為幼熊。

3 Bears live in <u>dens</u>. 熊住在洞穴裡。

4 The giant <u>panda</u> lives in China. 熊貓住在中國。

B 牠們住在哪裡？圈出正確的單字，並填入空格中。

1 The polar bear lives near the _____**North Pole**_____. 北極熊住在北極圈附近。
   (North Pole) South Pole

2 The sun bear lives in _____**rainforests**_____. 馬來熊住在雨林裡。
   deserts (rainforests)

3 The giant panda lives in _____**China**_____. 熊貓住在中國。
   (China) Chile

4 The grizzly bear lives in _____**North America**_____. 灰棕熊住在北美洲。
   (North America) South America

111

Unit 06 Earthquakes

地震

Reading Focus 閱讀焦點

- What is an earthquake? 何謂地震？
- What is a tsunami? 何謂海嘯？
- How are earthquakes dangerous? 地震是如何的危險？

Key Words 關鍵字彙

Earthquake
地震

ground
地面

ocean floor
海底

shaking
搖晃

large sea wave
大浪

cracks
裂縫；裂痕

tsunami
海嘯

huge damage
很大的損害（失）

Richter scale
芮氏地震分等標準

Power Verbs 核心動詞

shake
搖晃

The ground **shakes**.
地面在搖晃。

happen
發生

Earthquakes often **happen**.
地震時常發生。

make cracks
造成裂縫

Earthquakes **make cracks** in the ground.
地震在地面造成裂縫。

destroy
摧毀；毀壞

Earthquakes can **destroy** buildings.
地震會摧毀建築物。

kill
扼殺；殺害

Earthquakes can **kill** people.
地震會殘害人們。

cause
造成

An earthquake can **cause** a tsunami.
地震會造成海嘯。

hit
打擊；襲擊

A huge tsunami **hit** Japan.
大海嘯侵襲日本。

measure
測量

The earthquake **measured** 9.5.
這次地震被測出 9.5 級。

Earthquakes 地震

隆隆！地面搖晃了起來，
地面上所有的東西也跟著搖晃，
這就是地震。

地震每天都在發生，
但是大部分的地震都很小，
人們根本不會感覺到這些地震。

有些地震很強烈，
強烈地震會造成地面裂縫，
摧毀建築物，
也會奪走人類的性命。

有些地震發生在海底，
這些地震常常會掀起滔天巨浪，
這種現象稱為海嘯。
海嘯會造成重大的損失。

2011 年日本發生大地震，
大海嘯侵襲日本東北部，
奪走了成千上萬人的生命。

2004 年，也有巨大的海嘯襲捲印尼，
造成 20 餘萬人死亡。

目前最大的地震發生在 1960 年，
發生在智利，
芮式規模 9.5。

Chapter 2
Unit 06
Earthquakes

Check Understanding 文意測驗

1 下列圖片中分別是什麼事件？
   a <u>earthquake</u> 地震   **b** <u>tsunami</u> 海嘯

2 地震有多常發生？ **a**
   a 每天   **b** 一個禮拜一次   **c** 一個月一次

3 何謂海嘯？ **b**
   a 強烈的地震   **b** 滔天的巨浪   **c** 強大的暴風雨

4 目前最大的地震發生在_____。 **c**
   a 印尼   **b** 日本   **c** 智利

● 回答問題

1 What can earthquakes do? 地震會造成什麼？
   ⇨ They can make <u>cracks</u> in the ground and <u>destroy</u> buildings.
      地震造成地面裂縫，還會摧毀建築物。

2 What happened in 2011? 2011 年發生了什麼事？
   ⇨ A <u>huge</u> <u>tsunami</u> hit northeastern Japan. 大海嘯侵襲日本東北部。

Vocabulary and Grammar Builder 字彙與文法練習

Ⓐ 看圖填空：依照圖片選出正確的單字。
   1 An earthquake <u>shakes</u> the ground. 地震使地面搖晃。
   2 An underwater earthquake can cause a <u>tsunami</u>. 海底的地震會造成海嘯。
   3 A tsunami can <u>cause</u> huge damage. 海嘯會造成重大的損失。
   4 A large tsunami hit <u>Indonesia</u> in 2004. 2004 年，巨大的海嘯席捲印尼。

Ⓑ 可數或不可數：圈出正確的單字，並填入空格中。
   1 A tsunami is a ___**large**___ sea wave. 海嘯是滔天的巨浪。
      small (large)
   2 Some earthquakes kill ___**many**___ people. 有些地震會奪走人類的性命。
      much (many)
   3 ___**Most**___ earthquakes are very small. 大部分的地震都很小。
      (Most) Much
   4 ___**Many**___ earthquakes cause a large tsunami. 很多地震會造成大海嘯。
      (Many) Much

Unit 07 The Food Pyramid

食物金字塔

Reading Focus 閱讀焦點

• What is the food pyramid? 何謂食物金字塔？

• What are some grains? 穀類有哪些？

• What makes your muscles strong? 什麼讓你的肌肉強壯？

Key Words 關鍵字彙

The Five Food Groups
五大類食物

grains 穀物

vegetables 蔬菜類

fruits 水果

milk 奶類

meat 肉類

Food Gives Us 食物供給我們

energy 能量

strong bones 強健的骨骼

strong muscles 強壯的肌肉

Power Verbs 核心動詞

come from 來自於……

Milk **comes from** cows.
牛奶來自於乳牛。

include 包含

Grains **include** rice and bread.
穀物包括米和麵包。

give energy 給予能量

Food **gives energy** to your body.
食物給予你的身體能量。

keep 保持

Milk **keeps** you healthy.
牛奶使你保持健康。

Word Families: The Five Food Groups 相關字彙：五大類食物

grains 穀物

rice, wheat, bread
米飯、小麥、麵包

vegetables 蔬菜類

carrot, lettuce, tomato
胡蘿蔔、萵苣、蕃茄

fruits 水果

apple, banana, strawberry
蘋果、香蕉、草莓

milk 奶類

milk, cheese, yogurt
牛奶、起司、優格

meat 肉類

chicken, pork, beef, fish, egg, bean
雞肉、豬肉、牛肉、魚肉、雞蛋、豆類

The Food Pyramid　食物金字塔

你最喜歡的食物是什麼？
你喜歡吃肉嗎？你喜歡吃水果嗎？

食物來自於植物和動物。
穀物、水果和蔬菜都來自植物，
雞蛋、牛奶、魚肉和肉類都取自動物。

這是食物金字塔，
食物金字塔裡有五大類食物，
有穀類、蔬菜類、水果類、奶類和肉與豆類。
油並不算是一個食物類別，但你的身體需要
一些油來維持健康。

穀類食物像是米飯和麵包，
蔬菜類食物像是胡蘿蔔和萵苣，
水果類食物像是蘋果和香蕉，
奶類食物包括起司和優格，
肉與豆類包括魚肉、雞蛋和豆類。

穀物、蔬菜和水果會給予身體能量，
牛奶保持骨骼強壯，
肉類和魚肉保持肌肉強健。

食物金字塔是健康飲食的指標，
所有的食物類別都延伸至金字塔頂端，
這代表每一種食物類別都同等重要。

看一下金字塔裡每類食物的寬度，
這代表每樣食物最好攝取的份量，
最大的類別是穀類，
接著是蔬菜類、奶類、水果類、肉與豆類，
最後是油。
在金字塔的左邊，有一個人在爬樓梯，
這代表你需要每天運動，
這樣會讓你的身體健康。

Check Understanding　文意測驗

1 下列圖片中分別是哪一類的食物？
　　a milk 奶類　　　　　　**b** grains 穀類

2 穀物從哪裡來？ **a**
　　a 植物　　　　**b** 動物　　　　**c** 牛奶

3 肉類和魚肉使你的_____強健。　**c**
　　a 能量　　　　**b** 骨骼　　　　**c** 肌肉

● 回答問題

1 What food groups are on the food pyramid?　食物金字塔中有哪幾類食物？
　⇨ They are **grains**, **vegetables**, **fruits**, milk, and **meat and beans**.
　　有穀類、蔬菜類、水果類、奶類和肉與豆類。

2 What is the food pyramid?　何謂食物金字塔？
　⇨ It is a guide for **healthy** **eating**.　食物金字塔是健康飲食的指標。

Vocabulary and Grammar Builder　字彙與文法練習

Ⓐ 看圖填空：依照圖片選出正確的單字。

1 Eggs and meat come from **animals**.　雞蛋和肉類都取自動物。

2 **Grains** and vegetables come from plants.　穀物和蔬菜都來自植物。

3 Food gives us **energy**.　食物給我們能量。

4 The food pyramid is a **guide** for healthy eating.　飲食金字塔是健康飲食的指標。

Ⓑ 五大類食物：圈出正確的單字，並填入空格中。

1 Rice and bread are _____**grains**_____.　米飯和麵包都是穀物。
　　(grains) vegetables

2 Apples and bananas are ___**fruits**___.　蘋果和香蕉都是水果。
　　meat (fruits)

3 ___**Milk**___ includes cheese and yogurt.　奶類包括起司和優格。
　　Grain (Milk)

4 Carrots are _____**vegetables**_____.　胡蘿蔔是蔬菜類。
　　fruits (vegetables)

Staying Healthy

永保健康

Reading Focus 閱讀焦點

- How can we stay healthy? 我們要如何保持健康？
- How can we stay safe? 我們要如何保持安全？

Key Words 關鍵字彙

Staying Healthy
保持健康

healthy foods
健康的食物

keeping clean
保持乾淨

exercise
運動

being safe outdoors
在戶外保持安全

seatbelt
安全帶

baby seat
兒童座椅

Keeping Safe
保持安全

helmet
安全帽

following rules
遵守規矩

Power Verbs 核心動詞

stay healthy
保持健康

Eat healthy foods to **stay healthy**.
攝取健康的食物可以保持健康。

brush
刷（牙）

Brush your teeth every day.
每天都要刷牙。

exercise
運動

Exercise regularly.
規律地運動。

fight
對抗

Exercise helps you **fight** diseases.
運動幫助你對抗疾病。

follow
遵守

Follow the rules.
遵守規矩

wear
穿；戴；繫

Wear your seatbelt in a car.
坐車時，記得繫上安全帶。

Word Families 相關字彙

healthy foods
健康的食物

unhealthy foods
不健康的食物

restroom
廁所

safe
安全的

dangerous
危險的

outdoors
戶外

Staying Healthy 永保健康

今天，我們班看了關於健康生活的影片，
你可以用很多方法來保持健康。

首先，吃健康的食物，
攝取健康的食物幫助你成長得更強壯，
吃不健康的食物會讓你生病。

第二，時時刻刻保持乾淨，
保持乾淨會幫你保持健康，
永遠記得在以下時間洗手：
· 吃東西前
· 上完廁所
· 在外面玩完之後

一天至少刷兩次牙，
早上刷一次，
晚上睡前也要刷。

第三，規律的運動，
運動幫助你保持身體強壯，
也能幫助身體對抗疾病。

最後，在戶外保持安全，
我們可以在戶外做很多事，
但是一定要小心。

當你在戶外時，遵守以下規則：
· 騎腳踏車時，要戴安全帽。
· 坐車時，要繫安全帶。
· 運動時，遵守規則。

Check Understanding 文意測驗

1 下列圖片中分別在做些什麼？
   a **brushing teeth** 刷牙   **b** **exercise/exercising** 運動

2 什麼時候應該洗手？ **a**
   a 吃東西前   **b** 正在吃東西時   **c** 上廁所前

3 運動幫助你的身體對抗_____。**b**
   a 廁所   **b** 疾病   **c** 安全帶

4 騎腳踏車時，要戴_____。 **b**
   a 安全帶   **b** 安全帽   **c** 手套

● 回答問題

1 How often should you brush your teeth? 應該多久刷一次牙？
   ⇨ You should brush your teeth at least <u>twice a day</u>. 一天應該要至少刷兩次牙。

2 What should you do when you play sports? 當你運動時，應該要做什麼？
   ⇨ You should <u>follow the rules</u>. 應該要遵守規則。

Vocabulary and Grammar Builder 字彙與文法練習

Ⓐ 看圖填空：依照圖片選出正確的單字。

1 <u>Unhealthy</u> foods can make you sick. 不健康的食物會讓你生病。
2 Wash your hands after playing <u>outside</u>. 在外面玩以後要洗手。
3 Wear a <u>helmet</u> when you ride a bike. 騎腳踏車時，要戴安全帽。
4 Wear your <u>seatbelt</u> in a car. 坐車時，要繫安全帶。

Ⓑ V-ing：圈出正確的單字，並填入空格中。

1 ___**Eat**___ healthy foods. 攝取健康的食物。
   (Eat) Eating

2 ___**Eating**___ healthy foods helps you grow strong. 攝取健康的食物幫助你成長得更強壯。
   Eat (Eating)

3 Always ___**keep**___ yourself clean. 時時刻刻保持乾淨。
   (keep) keeping

4 ___**Keeping**___ clean helps you stay healthy. 保持乾淨會幫你保持健康。
   Keep (Keeping)

117

Where Is It?

在哪兒呢？

Reading Focus　閱讀焦點

- Can you use some words of position?　你會使用標明位置的用詞嗎？
- Where are the things in your room?　你房裡的東西分別放在哪兒呢？

Key Words 關鍵字彙

Where Is It?
在哪兒呢？

in
在……裡面

The pencils are **in** the pencil case.
鉛筆在鉛筆盒裡。

on
在……上面

The lamp is **on** the desk.
燈在桌上。

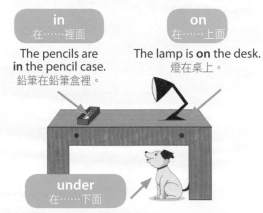

under
在……下面

The dog is **under** the desk.
狗在桌子下面。

Power Verbs 核心動詞

clean up
清理；整理

Clean up your room.
整理你的房間。

put
放（進）

Put the pencils in the
pencil case.
把鉛筆放進鉛筆盒。

Word Families 相關字彙

messy
髒亂的；混亂的

tidy = clean
整齊的 = 乾淨的；清潔的

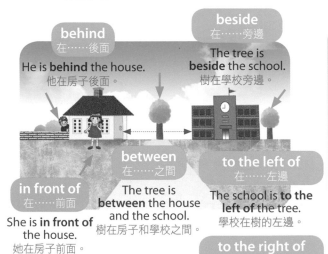

behind
在……後面

He is **behind** the house.
他在房子後面。

beside
在……旁邊

The tree is
beside the school.
樹在學校旁邊。

in front of
在……前面

She is **in front of**
the house.
她在房子前面。

between
在……之間

The tree is
between the house
and the school.
樹在房子和學校之間。

to the left of
在……左邊

The school is **to the
left of** the tree.
學校在樹的左邊。

to the right of
在……右邊

The tree is **to the right
of** the school.
樹在學校的右邊。

Things in Mary's Room
瑪麗房裡的東西

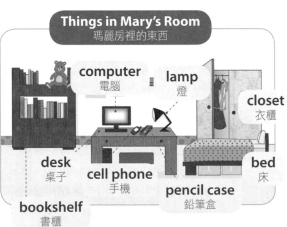

computer
電腦

lamp
燈

closet
衣櫃

desk
桌子

cell phone
手機

bed
床

bookshelf
書櫃

pencil case
鉛筆盒

Where Is It? 在哪兒呢？

瑪麗的媽媽說：「瑪麗，你的房間太亂了。」
「現在馬上清乾淨！」
「好吧。」瑪麗回答。
「我會把鉛筆放回鉛筆盒，
然後我會把書放在書櫃上。」
她的媽媽說：「妳的衣服都丟在地上，把它們放進衣櫥裡。」
「好吧。」瑪麗回答，「我還會把這些箱子都收進我的床底下。」
「還有這個燈應該是放在桌上的。」她媽媽說。
「好，媽媽，現在我的房間看起來如何？」瑪麗問。
「好多了。」她的媽媽回答道。

現在瑪麗的房間整齊了，
鉛筆都在鉛筆盒裡，

書都放在書櫃上，
衣服都收進衣櫥，
燈也擺在桌上了，
還有那些箱子也都收進床底下。

你看到那支手機了嗎？
就在鉛筆盒旁邊，
鉛筆盒在手機及燈之間。

衣櫥在桌子的左邊嗎？
不，衣櫥在桌子的右邊。
而且床在衣櫥的前面。

Check Understanding 文意測驗

1 看看下列圖片，書和床分別在哪裡？
   a The books are **on** the bookshelf. 書都在書櫃上。
   b The bed is **in front of** the closet. 床在衣櫥的前面。

2 瑪麗的房間有什麼不對？ **c**
   a 很乾淨。　　　　　**b** 很小。　　　　　**c** 很亂。

3 瑪麗把燈放在哪裡？ **a**
   a 桌上　　　　　**b** 桌子裡面　　　　　**c** 桌子下面

4 _____在衣櫥的前面。 **b**
   a 鉛筆　　　　　**b** 床　　　　　**c** 椅子

● 回答問題

1 Where does Mary put her clothes? 瑪麗把衣服放在哪裡？
   ⇨ She puts her clothes **in** the **closet**. 她把衣服放進衣櫥裡。

2 Where are the boxes? 那些箱子在哪裡？
   ⇨ The boxes are **under** the **bed**. 箱子在床底下。

Vocabulary and Grammar Builder 字彙與文法練習

Ⓐ 看圖填空：依照圖片選出正確的單字。
   1 Mary's room was too **messy**. 瑪麗的房間太亂了。
   2 Mary's room is **tidy** now. 現在瑪麗的房間整齊了。
   3 Mary puts the books on the **bookshelf**. 瑪麗把書放在書櫃上。
   4 Mary puts the **cell phone** beside the pencil case. 瑪麗把手機放在鉛筆盒旁邊。

Ⓑ 單字選填：圈出正確的單字，並填入空格中。
   1 The cell phone is _____**beside**_____ the pencil case. 手機在鉛筆盒旁邊。
      (beside) between
   2 The pencils are ___**in**___ the pencil case. 鉛筆都在鉛筆盒裡。
      (in) on
   3 The pencil case is ___**between**___ the cell phone and the lamp. 鉛筆盒在手機及燈之間。
      on (between)
   4 The bed is _____**in front of**_____ the closet. 床在衣櫥的前面。
      (in front of) behind

119

Unit 10 Addition and Subtraction

加法和減法

Reading Focus 閱讀焦點

• Can you add two numbers? 你可以把兩個數字加起來嗎？

• Can you subtract one number from another? 你可以把一個數字減掉另一個數字嗎？

• What are some symbols we use in math? 在數學中我們常用到的符號有哪些？

Key Words 關鍵字彙

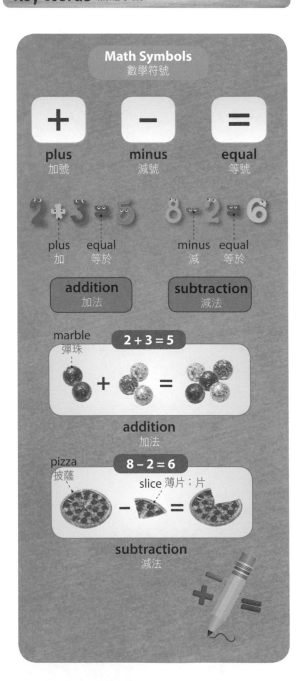

Math Symbols 數學符號

+ plus 加號　**–** minus 減號　**=** equal 等號

2 + 3 = 5
plus 加　equal 等於

8 – 2 = 6
minus 減　equal 等於

addition 加法　subtraction 減法

marble 彈珠
2 + 3 = 5
addition 加法

pizza 披薩
slice 薄片；片
8 – 2 = 6
subtraction 減法

Power Verbs 核心動詞

play with 玩……

He is **playing with** marbles.
他正在玩彈珠。

put together 放在一起

Let's **put** two numbers **together**.
讓我們把兩個數字放在一起。

2 + 3
add 加

Can you **add** two and three?
你可以把二跟三加起來嗎？

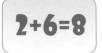

2 + 6 = 8
equal 等於……

Two plus six **equals** eight.
二加六等於八。

order 訂……；點餐

We **ordered** a pizza.
我們訂了一個披薩。

9 – 4 = 5
subtract 減法

Let's **subtract** four from nine.
我們把九減掉四。

Word Families: Plus and Minus
相關字彙：加與減

2 + 1 = 3 ➡ Two **plus** one **equals** three.
二加一等於三。

5 + 6 = 11 ➡ Five **plus** six **equals** eleven.
五加六等於十一。

4 – 3 = 1 ➡ Four **minus** three **equals** one.
四減三等於一。

9 – 7 = 2 ➡ Nine **minus** seven **equals** two.
九減七等於二。

Addition and Subtraction 加法和減法

喬和史蒂芬正在玩他們的彈珠，
喬有三個彈珠，史蒂芬有四個彈珠。
他們把彈珠放在一起，
現在總共有幾個彈珠？
總共有七個彈珠。

這就是加法，
把 3 跟 4 兩個數字加起來，
我們可以寫成這樣：
3 + 4 = 7
唸成：「三加四等於七。」

蘇有兩枝筆，克萊兒有六枝筆，
她們總共有幾枝筆？
她們有八枝筆。

把 2 跟 6 兩個數字加起來，
2 + 6 = 8
唸成：「二加六等於八。」

戴夫訂了一個披薩。
一個披薩有八片，
戴夫吃了兩片，
還剩下幾片？
還剩下六片。

這就是減法，
將 8 減掉 2，
可以寫成：
8 - 2 = 6
唸作：「八減二等於六。」

Check Understanding 文意測驗

1 下列圖片中分別是什麼？

a **subtraction** 減法   b **addition** 加法

2 哪一個符號用來將兩個數字加起來？ **a**

a +   b -   c =

3 四加二等於多少？ **c**

a 二   b 五   c 六

4 八_____二等於六。 **b**

a 加上   b 減掉   c 和

● 回答問題

1 How do you say 4 + 5 = 9? 4 + 5 = 9 怎麼唸？
⇨ Four **plus** five **equals** nine. 四加五等於九。

2 How do you say 10 – 3 = 7? 10 – 3 = 7 怎麼唸？
⇨ Ten **minus** three **equals** seven. 十減三等於七。

Vocabulary and Grammar Builder 字彙與文法練習

Ⓐ 看圖填空：依照圖片選出正確的單字。

1 They are **playing** with marbles.   他們正在玩彈珠。

2 Let's **order** a pizza.   我們來訂個披薩吧。

3 Can you **add** 2 and 6?   你可以把 2 跟 6 加起來嗎？

4 Can you **subtract** 2 from 8?   你可以將 8 減掉 2 嗎？

Ⓑ 計算：圈出正確的單字，並填入空格中。

1 Five ___**plus**___ seven equals twelve.   五加七等於十二。
(plus) minus

2 Eight ___**minus**___ three equals five.   八減三等於五。
plus (minus)

3 Two plus two ___**equals**___ four.   二加二等於四。
equal (equals)

4 Seven minus six equals ___**one**___.   七減六等於一。
(one) two

121

Unit 11 Sculptures

雕塑藝術

Reading Focus 閱讀焦點

• What is a sculpture? 何謂雕塑藝術？

• What are some famous sculptures? 有哪些有名的雕像？

• Who are some famous sculptors? 有哪些有名的雕刻家？

Key Words 關鍵字彙

Sculptures
雕像；雕塑品

sculpture
雕塑品

statue
雕像

mobile
平衡吊掛雕塑

Sculptures Are Made Of
雕塑的原料

stone
石頭

clay
黏土

wood
木頭

metal
金屬

sculptor
雕刻家

artist
藝術家

Power Verbs 核心動詞

be called
被稱為……

It **is called** a sculpture.
它被稱為雕像。

be made of
由……製成

It **is made of** stone.
它是由石頭製成。

create
創造

Sculptors **create** sculptures.
雕刻家創造雕塑品。

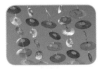

move
移動

It is **moving** in the wind.
它隨風飄動。

hang
把……掛起；掛

Hang the mobile from the ceiling.
把平衡吊掛雕塑掛在天花板上。

blow
（風）吹；吹動

The wind **blows**.
風在吹。

Word Families 相關字彙

as small as
像……一樣小

It is **as small as** your thumb.
它像你的拇指一樣小。

as big as
像……一樣大

It is **as big as** the tree.
它像樹一樣大。

Sculptures 雕塑藝術

看看這些圖片。

它們都是雕像，
它們也被稱為雕塑品。

雕塑品是由石頭、木頭或金屬所製成。
有些雕塑品很大，
其中一件最有名的雕塑品就是自由女神像，
它是一座很大的雕像，
大到人可以在裡面走動。

有些雕塑品很小，
它們可以像拇指一樣小。

你知道是誰製作了這些雕塑品嗎？
雕刻家製作雕塑品，
他們是藝術家，
創作了許多種類的雕塑藝術。

你知道有些雕塑品可以動嗎？
它們被稱為平衡吊掛雕塑。
這是一種動態雕塑品，
你可以將它掛在半空中，
當風吹來，他會隨風搖曳。

Check Understanding 文意測驗

1 下列圖片中分別是什麼？
   a the **Statue** of Liberty 自由女神像   **b** **mobile** 平衡吊掛雕塑

2 雕像又稱為什麼？ **a**
   a 雕塑品   **b** 畫作   **c** 平衡吊掛雕塑

3 雕刻家製作什麼？ **b**
   a 繪畫   **b** 雕塑品   **c** 圖畫

4 平衡吊掛雕塑是_____雕塑品。 **b**
   a 畫的   **b** 可以動的   **c** 做出來的

● 回答問題

1 What are sculptures made of? 雕塑品是由什麼製作的？
   ⇨ They are made of **stone**, **wood**, or **metal**. 它們是由石頭、木頭或金屬製成。

2 What is a famous sculpture? 有什麼有名的雕塑品？
   ⇨ The **Statue** of **Liberty** is a famous sculpture. 自由女神像是很有名的雕塑品。

Vocabulary and Grammar Builder 字彙與文法練習

A 看圖填空：依照圖片選出正確的單字。

1 A **sculptor** is an artist. 雕刻家是藝術家。

2 Sculptors create **sculptures**. 雕刻家創作雕塑藝術。

3 Some sculptures are as small as your **thumb**. 有些雕塑品像拇指一樣小。

4 A mobile moves when the wind **blows**. 平衡吊掛雕塑會隨風搖曳。

B 主動語態與被動語態：圈出正確的單字，並填入空格中。

1 Statues are also ___called___ sculptures. 雕像也被稱作雕塑品。
   call (called)

2 Sculptures are ___made___ of stone, wood, or metal. 雕塑品是由石頭、木頭或金屬所製成。
   make (made)

3 Mobiles are ___moving___ sculptures. 平衡吊掛雕塑就是可以動的雕塑品。
   (moving) moved

4 You can ___hang___ a mobile in the air. 你可以將平衡吊掛雕塑掛在半空中。
   (hang) hanging

Unit 12

A World of Instruments
樂器的世界

Reading Focus　閱讀焦點

- What are some traditional musical instruments?　傳統的樂器有哪些？
- How do these musical instruments sound?　這些樂器的聲音是怎麼樣的？

Key Words 關鍵字彙

Traditional Musical Instruments
傳統樂器

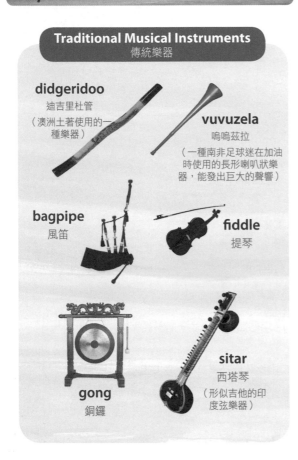

didgeridoo
迪吉里杜管
（澳洲土著使用的一種樂器）

vuvuzela
嗚嗚茲拉
（一種南非足球迷在加油時使用的長形喇叭狀樂器，能發出巨大的聲響）

bagpipe
風笛

fiddle
提琴

gong
銅鑼

sitar
西塔琴
（形似吉他的印度弦樂器）

 **folk music** 民俗音樂

Power Verbs 核心動詞

play
演奏

People **play** musical instruments.
人們演奏樂器。

be similar to
與……類似

It **is similar to** the didgeridoo.
它與迪吉里杜管類似。

make a sound
製造聲響

It **makes a sound** like an elephant.
它發出的聲音好像大象。

sound like
聽起來像……

The bagpipe **sounds like** a horn.
風笛的聲音聽起來像號角。

be like
跟……很像

A fiddle **is like** a violin.
提琴跟小提琴很像。

be used for
被用於……

The sitar **is used for** classical music.
西塔琴被用於古典音樂。

Word Families: The Three Groups of Music Instruments
相關字彙：三大類樂器

wind instrument
管樂器
→ horn・didgeridoo・vuvuzela
號角；小號・迪吉里杜管・嗚嗚茲拉

string instrument
弦樂器
→ violin・fiddle・sitar
小提琴・提琴・西塔琴

percussion instrument
打擊樂器
→ drum・gong
鼓・銅鑼

124

A World of Instruments 樂器的世界

很多人喜歡唱歌、跳舞，
他們隨著音樂歌唱和起舞。

在這世界上，人們演奏很多不同的樂器。
讓我們來看看。

在澳洲，有些人會吹奏迪吉里杜管，
那是一種又長又細的管樂器，
會發出一種嗡嗡的聲音。

在南非，有些人會吹奏嗚嗚茲拉，
它跟迪吉里杜管很像，
會發出很像大象的聲音。

在蘇格蘭，有些人會吹奏風笛，
它的聲音很像號角。

在美國，有些人會演奏提琴，
它跟小提琴很像，
但是人們用它來演奏民俗音樂。

在亞洲，有些人會敲擊銅鑼，
這是一種打擊樂器，
有許多種類。

在印度，有些人會彈奏西塔琴，
它是一種弦樂器，
用來演奏印度的傳統音樂。

Check Understanding 文意測驗

1 下列圖片中分別是哪一種樂器？
   a <u>vuvuzela</u> 嗚嗚茲拉　　　　**b** <u>bagpipe</u> 風笛

2 哪裡的人們會演奏迪吉里杜管？ **c**
   a 蘇格蘭　　　**b** 印度　　　**c** 澳洲

3 銅鑼屬於哪一種樂器？ **b**
   a 弦樂器　　　**b** 打擊樂器　　　**c** 管樂器

4 _____用來演奏印度的傳統音樂。 **c**
   a 銅鑼　　　**b** 嗚嗚茲拉　　　**c** 西塔琴

● 回答問題

1 What does the vuvuzela sound like?　嗚嗚茲拉的聲音聽起來像什麼？
   ⇨ It sounds like an <u>elephant</u>.　聽起來像大象。

2 What kind of music do people play on the fiddle?　人們用提琴來演奏什麼音樂？
   ⇨ They play <u>folk</u> <u>music</u>.　演奏民俗音樂。

Vocabulary and Grammar Builder 字彙與文法練習

Ⓐ 看圖填空：依照圖片選出正確的單字。

1 The bagpipe is played in <u>Scotland</u>.　風笛在蘇格蘭演奏。

2 The vuvuzela is <u>similar</u> to the didgeridoo.　嗚嗚茲拉跟迪吉里杜管很像。

3 A fiddle is <u>like</u> a violin.　提琴跟小提琴很像。

4 The didgeridoo makes a <u>buzzing</u> sound.　迪吉里杜管會發出一種嗡嗡的聲音。

Ⓑ 樂器：圈出正確的單字，並填入空格中。

1 The _____**didgeridoo**_____ is played in Australia.　迪吉里杜管在澳洲演奏。
   vuvuzela (didgeridoo)

2 The _____**vuvuzela**_____ is played in South Africa.　嗚嗚茲拉在南非演奏。
   (vuvuzela) didgeridoo

3 The ___**fiddle**___ is played in the United States.　提琴在美國演奏。
   sitar (fiddle)

4 The ___**gong**___ is played in Asia.　銅鑼在亞洲演奏。
   (gong) bagpipe

Ⓐ 看圖填空：依照圖片選出正確的單字。

1 About 1.39 **billion** people live in China.　大約有 13.9 億人口住在中國。

2 Mount Everest is in the **Himalayas**.　聖母峰屬於喜馬拉雅山脈。

3 Water and land are **natural resources**.　水和土地是天然資源。

4 We **recycle** paper and cans.　我們回收紙張和罐頭。

Ⓑ 圈出正確的單字，並填入空格中。

1 The United States is the ___**third**___ biggest country in the world.　美國是世界第三大的國家。
　　second (third)

2 The Andes ___**stretch**___ very long.　安地斯山脈綿延很長的距離。
　　rise (stretch)

3 People ___**breathe**___ air.　人類呼吸空氣。
　　drink (breathe)

4 Recycling can ___**save**___ natural resources.　回收可以節省天然資源。
　　(save) waste

Ⓒ 選出正確的單字，並填入空格中。

1 There are 193 **countries** in the world.　世界上有 193 個國家。

2 **Russia** is the biggest country in the world.　俄羅斯是世界上最大的國家。

3 China has the biggest **population** in the world.　中國是世界上人口最多的國家。

4 Every country has a **national anthem**.　每個國家都有國歌。

5 Mount **Everest** is the world's tallest mountain.　聖母峰是世界第一高峰。

6 The Andes Mountains are the world's longest **mountain range**.
　安地斯山脈是世界上連綿最長的山脈。

7 The world's largest desert is the **Sahara**.　撒哈拉沙漠是世界最大的沙漠。

8 The world's highest **waterfall** is Angel Falls.　天使瀑布是世界最高的瀑布。

Ⓓ 選出正確的單字，並填入空格中。

1 We **need** water to live.　我們需要水才能生存。

2 Without water, all **living things** cannot live.　沒有水，所有生物都無法存活。

3 We need to keep the water and air **clean**.　我們必須保持水和空氣乾淨。

4 If we do not save our natural resources, they will **disappear**.
　如果我們不珍惜天然資源，它們便會消失。

5 We can recycle, **reuse**, and reduce.　我們可以回收、再利用、減量。

6 Our class **collects** paper and cans.　我們班收集紙張和罐頭。

7 Recycling helps **save** natural resources.　回收會幫助留住天然資源。

8 When you leave a room, **turn off** the lights.　當我們離開房間，關上電燈。

A 看圖填空：依照圖片選出正確的單字。

1 A baby bear is called a <u>cub</u>. 小熊被稱為幼熊。

2 A tsunami can cause huge <u>damage</u>. 海嘯會造成重大的損失。

3 Food gives us <u>energy</u>. 食物給我們能量。

4 <u>Exercise</u> helps your body stay strong. 運動幫助身體保持強壯。

B 圈出正確的單字，並填入空格中。

1 The giant panda lives in ___China___. 熊貓住在中國。
Chile (China)

2 A tsunami is a ___large___ sea wave. 海嘯是滔天的巨浪。
small (large)

3 ___Grains___ include rice and bread. 穀物包括米飯和麵包。
(Grains) Fats

4 ___Eating___ unhealthy foods can make you sick. 吃不健康的食物會讓你生病。
Eat (Eating)

C 選出正確的單字，並填入空格中。

1 Bears have paws and sharp <u>claws</u>. 熊有熊掌和鋒利的爪子。

2 Bears have <u>fur</u> on their bodies. 熊身上覆蓋著毛皮。

3 The <u>polar bear</u> is the biggest bear in the world. 北極熊是世界上最大的熊。

4 Bears <u>sleep</u> during the winter. 熊冬天都在睡覺。

5 Big earthquakes can make <u>cracks</u> in the ground. 強烈地震會造成地面裂縫。

6 Earthquakes can <u>destroy</u> buildings 地震會摧毀建築物。

7 In 2011, a huge <u>tsunami</u> hit northeastern Japan. 2011 年，大海嘯侵襲日本東北部。

8 The biggest earthquake <u>measured</u> 9.5 on the Richter scale.
目前最大的地震是芮氏規模 9.5。

D 選出正確的單字，並填入空格中。

1 <u>Foods</u> come from plants and animals. 食物來自於植物及動物。

2 There are five food groups on the food <u>pyramid</u>. 食物金字塔中有五大類食物。

3 Grains include <u>rice</u> and bread. 穀類包含米飯和麵包。

4 The food pyramid is a <u>guide</u> for healthy eating. 食物金字塔是健康飲食的指標。

5 You can do many things to <u>stay</u> healthy. 你可以做很多事來保持健康。

6 Always <u>wash</u> your hands before you eat. 在吃東西前，一定要洗手。

7 Brush your teeth at least <u>twice</u> a day. 一天至少要刷兩次牙。

8 Follow the <u>rules</u> when you play sports. 當你運動時，要遵守規則。

Ⓐ 看圖填空：依照圖片選出正確的單字。

1　Mary's room was too **messy**.　瑪麗的房間太亂了。

2　Can you **subtract** 2 from 8?　你可以把 8 減掉 2 嗎？

3　Sculptors create **sculptures**.　雕刻家創造雕塑品。

4　People play **folk music** on a fiddle.　人們用提琴演民俗音樂。

Ⓑ 圈出正確的單字，並填入空格中。

1　The cell phone is _____**beside**_____ the pencil case.　手機在鉛筆盒的旁邊。
　　　　　　　　　　(beside)　between

2　Five ____**plus**____ eight equals thirteen.　五加八等於十三。
　　　(plus)　minus

3　Mobiles are _____**moving**_____ sculptures.　平衡吊掛雕塑就是可以動的雕塑品。
　　　　　　(moving)　moved

4　The didgeridoo is _____**played**_____ in Australia.　迪吉里杜管在澳洲演奏。
　　　　　playing　(played)

Ⓒ 選出正確的單字，並填入空格中。

1　Your clothes are **on** the floor.　你的衣服都丟在地上。

2　Put your clothes **in** the closet.　把你的衣服放進衣櫥。

3　The pencil case is **between** the cell phone and the lamp.　鉛筆盒在手機和桌燈之間。

4　Mary cleaned up her room. It is **tidy** now.　瑪麗整理完她的房間。房間現在整齊了。

5　We say, "Three plus four **equals** seven."　我們將此唸成：「三加四等於七。」

6　You **add** the two numbers 2 and 6.　將 2 和 6 兩個數字加起來。

7　You **subtract** 2 from 8.　將 8 減掉 2。

8　We say, "Eight **minus** two equals six."　我們將此唸成：「八減二等於六。」

Ⓓ 選出正確的單字，並填入空格中。

1　**Statues** are also called sculptures.　雕像也被稱為雕塑品。

2　Sculptures are **made** of stone, wood, or metal.　雕塑品是由石頭、木頭或是金屬製作而成。

3　Some sculptures can be as small as your **thumb**.　有些雕塑品可以像拇指一樣小。

4　You can hang a **mobile** in the air.　將平衡吊掛雕塑掛在半空中。

5　In Australia, some people play the **didgeridoo**.　在澳洲，有些人會吹奏迪吉里杜管。

6　The vuvuzela makes a sound like an **elephant**.　嗚嗚茲拉發出的聲音很像大象。

7　The gong is a **percussion** instrument.　銅鑼是打擊樂器。

8　The **sitar** is used for Indian classical music.　西塔琴用來演奏印度的傳統音樂。

Authors

Michael A. Putlack

Michael A. Putlack graduated from Tufts University in Medford, Massachusetts, USA, where he got his B.A. in History and English and his M.A. in History. He has written a number of books for children, teenagers, and adults.

e-Creative Contents

A creative group that develops English contents and products for ESL and EFL students.

FÜN學
美國各學科初級課本
新生入門英語閱讀 ④

作 者	Michael A. Putlack & e-Creative Contents
譯 者	陸葵珍
編 輯	賴祖兒／陸葵珍
主 編	丁宥暄
內文排版	謝青秀／林書玉
封面設計	林書玉
製程管理	洪巧玲
出版者	寂天文化事業股份有限公司
電 話	+886-(0)2-2365-9739
傳 真	+886-(0)2-2365-9835
網 址	www.icosmos.com.tw
讀者服務	onlineservice@icosmos.com.tw
出版日期	2023 年 5 月 二版三刷（寂天隨身聽 APP 版）

國家圖書館出版品預行編目資料

Fun學美國各學科初級課本：新生入門英語閱讀(寂天隨身聽APP版) / Michael A. Putlack, e-Creative Contents著. -- 二版. -- [臺北市] : 寂天文化, 2023.05-
　冊；　公分
ISBN 978-626-300-190-9 (第4冊：菊8K平裝)

1.CST: 英語 2.CST: 讀本

805.18　　　　　　　　　　112006028

FÜN學
美國各學科初級課本
新生入門英語閱讀 二版

AMERiCAN SCHOOL TEXTBOOK

Reading Key BASIC

4

WORKBOOK
練習本

Countries in the World

A Write the meaning of each word and phrase in Chinese.

1	country	_____	24	tiny	_____
2	in the world	_____	25	population	_____
3	how many	_____	26	only	_____
4	some	_____	27	about	_____
5	Russia	_____	28	live in	_____
6	the biggest	_____	29	billion	_____
7	the first	_____	30	1.39 billion	_____
8	Canada	_____	31	India	_____
9	the second	_____	32	more than	_____
10	the United States	_____	33	1.3 billion	_____
11	the third	_____	34	million	_____
12	China	_____	35	300 million	_____
13	Brazil	_____	36	every country	_____
14	the fourth	_____	37	its own	_____
15	the fifth	_____	38	flag	_____
16	the smallest	_____	39	national flag	_____
17	Vatican City	_____	40	national anthem	_____
18	be located	_____	41	follow	_____
19	inside	_____	42	the same	_____
20	Rome	_____	43	law	_____
21	Italy	_____	44	language	_____
22	bigger than	_____	45	culture	_____
23	city block	_____			

B Choose the word that best completes each sentence.

population	countries	block	laws

1 There are 193 _____ in the world.

2 Vatican City is no bigger than a city _____.

3 China has the biggest _____ in the world.

4 People in a country follow the same _____.

▶ B, C大題解答請參照主冊課文
　A大題解答請參照Word List（主冊P. 91）

Listen to the passage and fill in the blanks. 25

How many _____ are there in the world?

There are _____ countries in the world.

Some are big. _____ are small.

_____ is the biggest country in the world.

Canada is the _____ biggest country in the world.

The United States is the _____ biggest country in the world.

And China and Brazil are the fourth and _____ biggest countries.

What is the _____ country in the world?

It is _____ City.

It is located inside the city of _____, Italy.

It is no bigger than a city _____.

It has a _____ population, too.

Only about _____ people live in Vatican City.

Which country has the biggest _____?

China has the _____ population in the world.

About 1.39 _____ people live in China.

India has more than _____ billion people.

The United States has more than 300 _____ people.

Every country has its own _____.

It has a national _____, too.

People in a country follow the same _____.

They speak the same _____.

And they have the same _____.

4

A **Write the meaning of each word and phrase in Chinese.**

1 the best _____
2 around the world _____
3 some _____
4 low _____
5 others _____
6 high _____
7 Mount Everest _____
8 the world's tallest _____
9 rise _____
10 be located _____
11 the Himalayas _____
12 border _____
13 Nepal _____
14 call _____
15 top _____
16 the Andes (Mountains) _____
17 the world's longest _____
18 mountain range _____
19 stretch _____
20 South America _____
21 Europe _____
22 the Alps _____
23 Mont Blanc _____

24 the highest _____
25 peak _____
26 the Nile River _____
27 Africa _____
28 flow into _____
29 the Mediterranean Sea _____
30 the Amazon River _____
31 another _____
32 huge _____
33 across _____
34 the Atlantic Ocean _____
35 the world's largest _____
36 desert _____
37 the Sahara (Desert) _____
38 the Arabian Desert _____
39 the Middle East _____
40 the Gobi Desert _____
41 the world's highest _____
42 waterfall _____
43 Angel Falls _____
44 fall _____
45 Venezuela _____

B **Choose the word that best completes each sentence.**

waterfall	stretch	peak	rises

1 Mount Everest _____ 8,850 meters high.

2 The Andes Mountains _____ 7,000km long.

3 Mont Blanc is the highest _____ in the Alps.

4 The world's highest _____ is Angel Falls.

c **Listen to the passage and fill in the blanks.** 26

There are many _____ around the world.

Some are low. _____ are high.

Mount Everest is the world's _____ mountain.

It rises _____ meters high.

It is located in the _____ on the border of Nepal and China.

People call it "The Top of the _____."

The Andes Mountains are the world's longest mountain _____.

They _____ 7,000km long.

They are _____ in South America.

In Europe, there are the _____.

Mont Blanc is the highest _____ in the Alps.

The world's longest river is the _____ River.

It is in _____.

It _____ into the Mediterranean Sea.

The Amazon River is another _____ river.

It is _____ South America.

It flows across _____ to the Atlantic Ocean.

The world's largest _____ is the Sahara in Africa.

Next is the Arabian Desert in the _____ _____.

The _____ Desert in Asia is another huge desert.

The world's highest _____ is Angel Falls.

It _____ 807m.

It is in _____ in South America.

6

03 Earth Is Our Home

A Write the meaning of each word and phrase in Chinese.

1	earth	17	living thing
2	look at	18	air
3	picture	19	breathe
4	use	20	clean
5	need	21	need to
6	live	22	keep
7	drink	23	natural resource
8	grow	24	nature
9	food	25	land
10	wash clothes	26	important
11	cook food	27	fruit
12	plant	28	every day
13	also	29	should not
14	animal	30	waste
15	too	31	save
16	without	32	disappear

B Choose the word that best completes each sentence.

clothes	disappear	living	natural

1 We use water to wash _____ and to cook food.

2 Without water, all _____ things cannot live.

3 Air, water, and land are important _____ resources.

4 If we do not save our natural resources, they will _____.

Listen to the passage and fill in the blanks.

Look at the _____.
How are they _____ water?

We need _____ to live.
We use water to _____.
We use water to _____ food.
We use water to wash _____ and to cook food.

Plants also _____ water to grow.
And _____ need water to live, too.
Without water, all _____ _____ cannot live.

We need air to _____.
When the water and air are not _____, we cannot use them.
We need to _____ the water and air clean.

Water and air are natural _____.
Natural resources come from _____.
Air, water, and _____ are important natural resources.

Trees are _____ natural resource.
We make many things from _____.
We also use the _____ from trees.

_____ is our home.
We use natural resources _____ _____.
We should not _____ our natural resources.
If we do not _____ our natural resources, they will disappear.

8

Recycle, Reuse, and Reduce

A Write the meaning of each word and phrase in Chinese.

1	recycle	_____	18 plastic	_____
2	reuse	_____	19 glass	_____
3	reduce	_____	20 then	_____
4	our class	_____	21 put into	_____
5	learn	_____	22 recycling bin	_____
6	be learning	_____	23 be made into	_____
7	how to	_____	24 new things	_____
8	save	_____	25 again and again	_____
9	less	_____	26 both sides	_____
10	trash	_____	27 bag	_____
11	first	_____	28 box	_____
12	collect	_____	29 what we use	_____
13	every Monday	_____	30 brush one's teeth	_____
14	what	_____	31 turn off	_____
15	what our class collects	_____	32 leave a room	_____
16	paper	_____	33 light	_____
17	cans	_____		

B Choose the word that best completes each sentence.

turn off	save	recycle	collects

1 Our class is learning how to _____ natural resources.

2 We can _____, reuse, and reduce.

3 Our class _____ things every Monday.

4 When you leave a room, _____ the lights.

C Listen to the passage and fill in the blanks.

My name is _____.

Our class is _____ how to save natural resources.

We can recycle, _____, and reduce.

This makes less _____.

It also helps save natural _____.

First, we can _____ many things.

Our class _____ things every Monday.

Here is _____ our class collects.

We collect _____.

We collect _____.

We collect _____.

We collect _____.

Then, we put them into a _____ _____.

These things can be _____ into new things.

Then, we can use them again and _____.

We can _____ reuse paper.

We write on both _____.

We save bags and _____.

Then, we reuse _____.

We can also _____ what we use.

When you brush your _____, turn off the water.

When you leave a room, turn off the _____.

A World of Animals: Bears

A Write the meaning of each word and phrase in Chinese.

1 bear _____
2 fur _____
3 body _____
4 black _____
5 brown _____
6 white _____
7 paw _____
8 sharp _____
9 claw _____
10 baby bear _____
11 be called _____
12 cub _____
13 tiny _____
14 be born _____
15 drink milk _____
16 grow up _____
17 leave _____

18 den _____
19 hunt fish _____
20 polar bear _____
21 the North Pole _____
22 sun bear _____
23 rainforest _____
24 giant panda _____
25 brown bear _____
26 many parts of the world _____
27 grizzly bear _____
28 North America _____
29 late fall _____
30 find _____
31 winter home _____
32 sleep _____
33 during the winter _____
34 move _____

B Choose the word that best completes each sentence.

paws	fur	winter homes	cubs

1 Bears have _____ on their bodies.

2 Bears have _____ and sharp claws.

3 Bear _____ are tiny when they are born.

4 In the late fall, many bears find _____.

C **Listen to the passage and fill in the blanks.** 29

Look at the _____.

Bears have fur on their _____.

It can be black, brown, or _____.

Bears have _____ and sharp _____.

A baby bear is called a _____.

Bear cubs are _____ when they are born.

They drink _____ from their mothers.

When cubs grow up, they _____ their mothers.

Bears live in _____.

Bears eat all _____ food.

Some bears even _____ fish.

The _____ bear is the biggest bear in the world.

It lives near the _____ _____.

The sun bear is the smallest _____ in the world.

It lives in _____.

The _____ panda lives in China.

It has black and white _____.

The brown bear lives in many _____ _____ the world.

The grizzly bear _____ in North America.

In the late fall, many bears find winter _____.

They sleep _____ the winter.

They do not eat, drink, or _____ during the winter.

12

A Write the meaning of each word and phrase in Chinese.

1	earthquake	_____	14	cause	_____
2	rumble	_____	15	sea wave	_____
3	ground	_____	16	tsunami	_____
4	shake	_____	17	damage	_____
5	happen	_____	18	hit	_____
6	most	_____	19	northeastern	_____
7	feel	_____	20	Japan	_____
8	crack	_____	21	thousands of	_____
9	make cracks	_____	22	Indonesia	_____
10	destroy	_____	23	200,000 people	_____
11	kill	_____	24	Chile	_____
12	under	_____	25	measure	_____
13	ocean floor	_____	26	on the Richter scale	_____

B Choose the word that best completes each sentence.

> cracks   cause   tsunami   ocean floor

1 Big earthquakes can make _____ in the ground.

2 Some earthquakes happen under the _____.

3 Many of them _____ a large sea wave.

4 A huge _____ hit northeastern Japan.

Listen to the passage and fill in the blanks. 30

Rumble! The ground starts to _____.
Everything on the _____ shakes.
This is an _____.

Earthquakes _____ every day.
But _____ earthquakes are very small.
So people do not _____ these earthquakes.

Some _____ can be very big.
Big earthquakes can make _____ in the ground.
They can _____ buildings.
And they can _____ many people, too.

Some earthquakes happen under the ocean _____.
Many of them cause a large _____ _____.
This is called a _____.
A tsunami can cause huge _____.

In 2011, there was a big earthquake in _____.
A huge tsunami hit _____ Japan.
It killed _____ of people.

In 2004, a large tsunami hit _____, too.
It killed more than _____ people.

The biggest earthquake was in _____.
It happened in _____.
It measured 9.5 on the Richter _____.

The Food Pyramid

A Write the meaning of each word and phrase in Chinese.

1 food pyramid _____
2 favorite food _____
3 meat _____
4 come from _____
5 grains _____
6 fruits _____
7 vegetables _____
8 eggs _____
9 milk _____
10 fish _____
11 five food groups _____
12 oils _____
13 only _____
14 amount _____
15 in small amounts _____
16 like _____
17 rice _____

18 bread _____
19 carrot _____
20 lettuce _____
21 include _____
22 cheese _____
23 yogurt _____
24 bean _____
25 give energy _____
26 keep _____
27 bone _____
28 muscle _____
29 guide _____
30 healthy _____
31 reach _____
32 top _____
33 width _____
34 climb _____

B Choose the word that best completes each sentence.

guide	pyramid	come from	energy

1 Foods _____ plants and animals.

2 There are five food groups on the food _____.

3 Grains, vegetables, and fruits give _____ to your body.

4 The food pyramid is a _____ for healthy eating.

C Listen to the passage and fill in the blanks. 31

What's your _____ food?

Do you like _____? Do you like fruits?

Foods come from _____ and animals.

Grains, fruits, and _____ come from plants.

Eggs, _____, fish, and meat come from animals.

This is a food _____.

There are five _____ groups on the food pyramid.

They are grains, vegetables, _____, milk, and meat and beans.

_____ are not a food group, but you need some for good health.

Grains are foods like rice and _____.

Vegetables are foods like carrots and _____.

Fruits are _____ like apples and bananas.

Milk includes cheese and _____.

Meat and beans _____ fish, eggs, and beans.

_____, vegetables, and fruits give energy to your body.

Milk keeps your _____ strong.

Meat and fish make your _____ strong.

The food pyramid is a _____ for healthy eating.

All food groups _____ the top of the pyramid.

That means each kind of food is equally _____.

16

A Write the meaning of each word and phrase in Chinese.

1 stay _____

2 healthy _____

3 stay healthy _____

4 healthy living _____

5 healthy foods _____

6 unhealthy foods _____

7 sick _____

8 keep oneself clean _____

9 wash one's hands _____

10 at these times _____

11 restroom _____

12 play outside _____

13 brush one's teeth _____

14 at least _____

15 twice a day _____

16 go to bed _____

17 exercise _____

18 regularly _____

19 fight diseases _____

20 last _____

21 outdoors _____

22 careful _____

23 follow _____

24 rule _____

25 wear a helmet _____

26 ride a bike _____

27 wear one's seatbelt _____

28 play sports _____

B Choose the word that best completes each sentence.

unhealthy	stay	exercise	careful

1 You can do many things to _____ healthy.

2 Eating _____ foods can make you sick.

3 _____ helps your body stay strong.

4 We need to be _____ when we are outside.

C **Listen to the passage and fill in the blanks.**

Today, our class saw a _____ about healthy living.

You can do many things to _____ healthy.

First, eat _____ foods.

Eating healthy foods _____ you grow strong.

Eating _____ foods can make you sick.

Second, always keep _____ clean.

Keeping _____ helps you stay healthy.

Always wash your hands at these _____:

• Before _____

• After using the _____

• After _____ outside

Brush your teeth at least _____ a day.

_____ in the morning.

Brush before you go to _____ at night.

Third, exercise _____.

Exercise helps your body stay _____.

It also helps your body fight _____.

Last, be _____ outdoors.

We can do many things _____.

But we need to be _____.

Follow these rules when you are _____:

• Wear a _____ when you ride a bike.

• In a car, wear your _____.

• Follow the _____ when you play sports.

A Write the meaning of each word and phrase in Chinese.

1	room	_____	
2	too	_____	
3	messy	_____	
4	clean up	_____	
5	right now	_____	
6	put	_____	
7	pencil	_____	
8	in	_____	
9	pencil case	_____	
10	on	_____	
11	bookshelf	_____	
12	clothes	_____	
13	floor	_____	
14	closet	_____	

15 respond _____

16 under _____

17 bed _____

18 lamp _____

19 should be _____

20 How does…look? _____

21 much better _____

22 tidy _____

23 cell phone _____

24 beside _____

25 between _____

26 to the left of _____

27 to the right of _____

28 in front of _____

B Choose the word that best completes each sentence.

clean	messy	tidy	under

1 Mary, your room is too _____.

2 _____ it up right now.

3 I'll put these boxes _____ my bed.

4 Mary's room is _____ now.

"Mary, your room is too _____," says her mother.

"Clean it up _____ now."

"Okay," _____ Mary.

"I'll put the pencils in the _____ _____.

And I'll put the books on the _____."

Her mother says, "Your clothes are on the floor. Put them in the _____."

Mary responds, "Okay, and I will put these boxes _____ my bed."

"And the _____ should be on the desk," says her mother.

"Okay, Mom. How does my room _____ now?" Mary asks.

"It's much _____," her mother answers.

Mary's room is _____ now.

The _____ are in the pencil case.

The _____ are on the bookshelf.

The _____ are in the closet.

The lamp is _____ the desk.

And the boxes are under the _____.

Do you see the _____ _____?

It is _____ the pencil case.

The pencil case is _____ the cell phone and the lamp.

Is the closet to the _____ of the desk?

No, the closet is to the _____ of the desk.

And the bed is _____ _____ _____ the closet.

20

Addition and Subtraction

A **Write the meaning of each word and phrase in Chinese.**

1 addition _____
2 subtraction _____
3 play with _____
4 marble _____
5 put…together _____
6 add _____
7 like this _____
8 plus _____

9 equal _____
10 order _____
11 pizza _____
12 slice _____
13 be left _____
14 subtract _____
15 minus _____

B **Choose the word that best completes each sentence.**

addition	marbles	slices	plus
pizza	subtract	subtraction	minus

1 Joe and Steve are playing with their _____.

2 $3 + 4 = 7$. This is _____.

3 We say, "Three _____ four equals seven."

4 Dave orders a _____.

5 It has eight _____.

6 $8 - 2 = 6$. This is _____.

7 You _____ 2 from 8.

8 We say, "Eight _____ two equals six."

C Listen to the passage and fill in the blanks.

Joe and Steve are _____ with their marbles.

Joe has three marbles, and Steve has four _____.

They put their marbles _____.

How many marbles are _____ now?

There are _____ marbles.

This is _____.

You _____ the two numbers 3 and 4.

We can _____ it like this:

3 + _____ = 7.

We say, "Three plus four _____ seven."

Sue has two pens, and Clara has six _____.

How _____ pens do they have together?

They have _____ pens.

You add the two _____ 2 and 6.

2 + 6 = _____.

We say, "Two _____ six equals eight."

Dave _____ a pizza.

It has eight _____.

Dave eats _____ slices.

How many slices are _____?

There are _____ slices now.

This is _____.

You _____ 2 from 8.

We can write it like _____ :

_____ – 2 = 6.

We say, "Eight _____ two equals six."

Sculptures

A Write the meaning of each word and phrase in Chinese.

1 sculpture _____
2 look at _____
3 statue _____
4 be called _____
5 be made of _____
6 stone _____
7 wood _____
8 metal _____
9 famous _____
10 the Statue of Liberty _____
11 so…that… _____
12 inside _____

13 as small as _____
14 thumb _____
15 sculptor _____
16 artist _____
17 create _____
18 many kinds of _____
19 move _____
20 mobile _____
21 moving sculpture _____
22 hang _____
23 in the air _____
24 blow _____

B Choose the word that best completes each sentence.

sculptors	sculptures	mobile	Statue

1 _____ are made of stone, wood, or metal.

2 One of the most famous sculptures is the _____ of Liberty.

3 _____ are artists.

4 A _____ is a moving sculpture.

Look at these _____.

They are _____.
They are also called _____.

Sculptures are made of stone, wood, or _____.
Some sculptures are _____.
One of the most _____ sculptures is the Statue of Liberty.
It is a very big _____.
It is so big that people can walk _____ it.

Some sculptures are _____.
They can be _____ small _____ your thumb.

Do you know who _____ these sculptures?
_____ make these sculptures.
Sculptors are _____.
They _____ many kinds of sculptures.

Did you know that some sculptures can _____?
They are called _____.
A mobile is a _____ sculpture.
You can _____ a mobile in the air.
When the wind _____, the mobile moves.

A World of Instruments

A **Write the meaning of each word and phrase in Chinese.**

1 instrument _____
2 play _____
3 different _____
4 musical instrument _____
5 Australia _____
6 didgeridoo _____
7 thin _____
8 wind instrument _____
9 make a sound _____
10 buzzing sound _____
11 South Africa _____
12 vuvuzela _____
13 be similar to _____
14 elephant _____
15 Scotland _____
16 bagpipe _____

17 sound like _____
18 horn _____
19 the United States _____
20 fiddle _____
21 be like _____
22 violin _____
23 folk music _____
24 Asia _____
25 gong _____
26 percussion instrument _____
27 India _____
28 sitar _____
29 string instrument _____
30 be used for _____
31 Indian classical music _____

B **Choose the word that best completes each sentence.**

fiddle	vuvuzela	sitar	didgeridoo

1 In Australia, some people play the _____.

2 The _____ makes a sound like an elephant.

3 People play folk music on a _____.

4 The _____ is used for Indian classical music.

Many people _____ _____ sing and dance.

They sing and dance to _____.

Around the world, people play many different _____ instruments.

Let's look _____ some of them.

In _____, some people play the didgeridoo.

This is a long, thin _____ instrument.

It makes a _____ sound.

In South Africa, some people _____ the vuvuzela.

It is _____ to the didgeridoo.

It makes a _____ like an elephant.

In Scotland, some people play the _____.

It sounds like a _____.

In the United States, some people play the _____.

It is like the _____.

But people play _____ music on a fiddle.

In _____, some people play the gong.

It is a _____ instrument.

There are many _____ of gongs.

In _____, some people play the sitar.

It is a _____ instrument.

It is used for Indian _____ music.